ACT ONE

ACT ONE

A novella by

NANCY KRESS

PHOENIX PICK
an imprint of

ARC
MANOR
Rockville, Maryland

ISBN: 978-1-60450-455-2

www.PhoenixPick.com
Great Science Fiction at Great Prices

Visit the Author's Website at:
www.sff.net/people/nankress/

Published by Phoenix Pick
an imprint of Arc Manor
P. O. Box 10339
Rockville, MD 20849-0339
www.ArcManor.com

BREEDING FICTION
by Nancy Kress

STORIES CAN GROW OUT of anything: a fleeting thought, an overheard remark, a dream, a news item, a memory. Sometimes the writer has no idea where a particular story comes from. It just suddenly seems present, like air. Usually, however, stories grow from a combination of elements that arrive in the mind from different places and at different times. "Act One" is such a hybrid. Four germ cells cross-fertilized to produce it.

The first was my long-standing interest in genetic engineering, as well as a long-standing frustration that it is often written about so badly. Recombining genes will produce monsters without souls. No—it will produce supermen. No—it will produce a rigidly stratified society locked in by genetics, as in *Brave New World*. No—it will save humankind. No—it will be used for women to eliminate men, or blonds to eliminate redheads, or some mad scientist in a basement to eliminate everybody.

The much more likely scenario is that genetic engineering, like medicine and physics, will lurch forward in fits and starts. It will make some mistakes. It will create some benefits. It will have some unforeseen consequences. This is already happening, because a genome is not a destiny. A hundred other influences determine what turns genes on and off in a given individual, as the burgeoning science of epigenetics proves every day. So I wanted to write a story in which a deliberate change to the human genome results in ambiguous outcomes for multiple characters.

Such a goal is not a story, however. A story has specific characters and a specific situation. The second element that ultimately produced "Act One" was an image of two people groping their way down a grimy basement staircase. I didn't know anything about one of them, but I knew the second was a middle-aged woman of fragile beauty and iron will. She was an actress. I could see her quite clearly, although not why she was descending into that basement.

A few weeks later I was poking around the public library, scanning the shelf of NEW NON-FICTION. It held a book on dwarfism. The book seemed to be really well-written so I checked it out. After a few pages, I knew who the second person on the staircase was. Over the next few weeks I read two more books on dwarfism. Writers do this: read six times as much verbiage in research than the length of the eventual story. I read a book by a journalist, one by a dwarf, one by the average-sized father of a dwarf daughter. They were all fascinating.

The final piece of my story came during a chess match. I play a lot of chess, and I play it very badly. My usual chess partner, Marty, and I will play several games in a row, accompanied by chess trash talk ("Don't think that's a move that impresses me!" "You think I don't see the bishop moving up? In your dreams!") My toy poodle, Cosette, watches us distrustfully, and somehow she always knows when it's the last game of the evening, sometimes even before we do. How does she know? What clues is she reading?

Once Marty and I asked each other this question, the entire story of "Act One" solidified in my mind. I knew what genetic engineering change it would concern, to whom it would happen, why, and with what consequences. The actual writing then went swiftly.

Not all my stories are grown this way. Sometimes the soil is less fertile. Sometimes I just can't quite come up with enough inventive rain to keep the thing alive. Sometimes the result is puny and pale.

But, then, literary cross-breeding is just as chancy as the biological kind. And we lurch forward anyway.

"To understand whose movie it is one needs to look not particularly at the script but at the deal memo."

—*Joan Didion*

♈

ACT ONE

I EASED DOWN THE warehouse's basement steps behind the masked boy, one hand on the stair rail, wishing I'd worn gloves. Was this level of grime really necessary? It wasn't; we'd already passed through some very sophisticated electronic surveillance, as well as some very unsophisticated personal surveillance that stopped just short of a body-cavity search, although an unsmiling man did feel around inside my mouth. Soap cost less than surveillance, so probably the grime was intentional. The Group was making a statement. That's what we'd been told to call them: "The Group." Mysterious, undefined, pretentious.

The stairs were lit only by an old-fashioned forty-watt bulb somewhere I couldn't see. Behind me, Jane's breath quickened. I'd insisted on going down first, right behind our juvenile guide, from a sense of—what? "Masculine protection" from me would be laughable. And usually I like to keep Jane where I can see her. It works out better that way.

"Barry?" she breathed. The bottom of the steps was so shrouded in gloom that I had to feel my way with one extended foot.

"Two more steps, Janie."

"Thank you."

Then we were down and she took a deep breath, standing closer to me than she usually does. Her breasts were level with my face. Jane is only five-six, but that's seventeen inches taller than I am. The boy said, "A little way more."

Across the cellar a door opened, spilling out light. "There."

It had been a laundry area once, perhaps part of an apartment for some long-dead maintenance man. Cracked wash tubs, three of them, sagged in one corner. No windows, but the floor had been covered with a clean, thin rug and the three waiting people looked clean, too. I scanned them quickly. A tall, hooded man holding an assault rifle, his eyes the expression of bodyguards everywhere: alert but nonanalytic. An unmasked woman in jeans and baggy sweater, staring at Jane with unconcealed resentment. Potential trouble there. And the leader, who came forward with his hand extended, smiling. "Welcome, Miss Snow. We're honored."

I recognized him immediately. He was a type rampant in political life, which used to be my life. Big, handsome, too pleased with himself and his position to accurately evaluate either. He was the only one not wearing jeans, dressed in slacks and a sports coat over a black turtleneck. If he had been a pol instead of a geno-terrorist, he'd have maybe gotten as far as city council executive, and then would have run for mayor, lost, and never understood why. So this was a low-level part of the Group's operation, which was probably good. It might lessen the danger of this insane expedition.

"Thank you," Jane said in that famous voice, low and husky and as thrilling off screen as on. "This is my manager, Barry Tenler."

I was more than her manager but the truth was too

complicated to explain. The guy didn't even glance at me and I demoted him from city council executive to ward captain. You *always* pay attention to the advisors. That's usually where the brains are, if not the charisma.

Ms. Resentful, on the other hand, switched her scrutiny from Jane to me. I recognized the nature of that scrutiny. I've felt it all my life.

Jane said to the handsome leader, "What should I call you?"

"Call me Ishmael."

Oh, give me a break. Did that make Jane the white whale? He was showing off his intellectual moves, with no idea they were both banal and silly. But Jane gave him her heart-melting smile and even I, who knew better, would have sworn it was genuine. She might not have made a movie in ten years, but she still had it.

"Let's sit down," Ishmael said.

Three kitchen chairs stood at the far end of the room. Ishmael took one, the bodyguard and the boy standing behind him. Ms. Resentful took another. Jane sank cross-legged to the rug in a graceful puddle of filmy green skirt.

That was done for my benefit. My legs and spine hurt if I have to stand for more than a few minutes, and she knows how I hate sitting even lower than I already am. Ishmael, shocked and discerning nothing, said, "Miss Snow!"

"I think better when I'm grounded," she said, again with her irresistible smile. Along with her voice, that smile launched her career thirty-five years ago. Warm, passionate, but with an underlying wistfulness that bypassed the cerebrum and went straight to the primitive hind-brain. Unearned—she was born with those assets—but not unexploited. Jane was a lot shrewder than her fragile blonde looks suggested. The passion, however, was real. When she wanted something, she wanted it with every sinew, every nerve cell, every drop of her acquisitive blood.

Now her graceful Sitting-Bull act left Ishmael looking awkward on his chair. But he didn't do the right thing, which would have been to join her on the rug. He stayed on his chair and I demoted him even further, from ward captain to go-fer. I clambered up onto the third chair. Ishmael gazed down at Jane and swelled like a pouter pigeon at having her, literally, at his feet. Ms. Resentful scowled. Uneasiness washed through me.

The Group knew who Jane Snow was. Why would they put this meeting in the hands of an inept narcissist? I could think of several reasons: to indicate contempt for her world. To preserve the anonymity of those who actually counted in this most covert of organizations. To pay off a favor that somebody owed to Ishmael, or to Ishmael's keeper. To provide a photogenic foil to Jane, since of course we were being recorded. Any or all of these reasons would be fine with me. But my uneasiness didn't abate.

Jane said, "Let's begin then, Ishmael, if it's all right with you."

"It's fine with me," he said. His back was to the harsh light, which fell full on both Jane and Ms. Resentful. The latter had bad skin, small eyes, lanky hair, although her lips were lovely, full and red, and her neck above the windbreaker had the taut firmness of youth.

The light was harder on Jane. It showed up the crow's feet, the tired inelasticity of her skin under her flawless make-up. She was, after all, fifty-four, and she'd never gone under the knife. Also, she'd never been really beautiful, not as Angelina Jolie or Catherine Zeta-Jones had once been beautiful. Jane's features were too irregular, her legs and butt too heavy. But none of that mattered next to the smile, the voice, the green eyes fresh as new grass, and the powerful sexual glow she gave off so effortlessly. *It's as if Jane Snow somehow received two sets of female genes at conception*, a critic wrote once, *doubling everything we think of as "feminine." That makes her either a goddess or a freak.*

"I'm preparing for a role in a new movie," she said to Ishmael, although of course he already knew that. She just wanted to use her voice on him. "It's going to be about your... your organization. And about the future of the little girls. I've talked to some of them and—"

"Which ones?" Ms. Resentful demanded.

Did she really know them all by name? I looked at her more closely. Intelligence in those small, stony eyes. She could be from The Group's headquarter cell—wherever it was — and sent to ensure that Ishmael didn't screw up this meeting. Or not. But if she were really intelligent, would she be so enamored of someone like Ishmael?

Stupid question. Three of Jane's four husbands had been gorgeous losers.

Jane said, "Well, so far I've only talked to Rima Ridley-Jones. But Friday I have the whole afternoon with the Barrington twins."

Ishmael, unwilling to have the conversation migrate from him, said, "Beautiful children, those twins. And very intelligent." As if the entire world didn't already know that. Unlike most of The Group's handiwork, the Barrington twins had been posed by their publicity-hound parents on every magazine cover in the world. But Jane smiled at Ishmael as if he'd just explicated Spinoza.

"Yes, they are beautiful. Please, Ishmael, tell me about your organization. Anything that might help me prepare for my role in *Future Perfect*."

He leaned forward, hands on his knees, handsome face intent. Dramatically, insistently, he intoned, "There is one thing you must understand about the Group, Jane. A very critical thing. *You will never stop us.*"

Portentous silence.

The worst thing was, he might be right. The FBI, CIA, IRS, HPA, and several other alphabets had lopped off a few heads, but still the hydra grew. It had so many supporters: liberal lawmakers and politicians, who wanted the Anti-Genetic Modification Act revoked and the Human Protection Agency dismantled. The rich parents who wanted their embryos enhanced. The off-shore banks that coveted The Group's dollars and the Caribbean or Mexican or who-knows-what islands that benefited from sheltering their mobile labs.

"We are idealists," Ishmael droned on, "and we are the future. Through our efforts, mankind will change for the better. Wars will end, cruelty will disappear. When people can—"

"Let me interrupt you for just a moment, Ishmael." Jane widened her eyes and over-used his name. Her dewy look up at him from the floor could have reversed desertification. She was pulling out all the stops. "I need so *much* to understand, Ishmael. If you genemod these little girls, one by one, you end up changing such a small percentage of the human race that... How many children have been engineered with Arlen's Syndrome?"

"We prefer the term 'Arlen's Advantage.'"

"Yes, of course. How many children?"

I held my breath. The Group had never given out that information.

Jane put an entreating hand on Ishmael's knee.

He said loftily, hungrily, "That information is classified," and I saw that he didn't know the answer.

pered, "I'm so sorry, Barry. But this was my only chance."

"I know." Somehow I made it up the stairs. We navigated the maze of the abandoned warehouse, where The Group's unseen soldiers stayed at stand-off with our own unseen bodyguards. Blinking in the sunlight, I suddenly collapsed onto the broken concrete.

"Barry!"

"It's…okay. *Don't*."

"The rest will be so much easier…I promise!"

I got myself upright, or what passes for upright. The unmarked van arrived for us. The whole insane interview had gone off without a hitch, without violence, smooth as good chocolate.

So why did I still feel so uneasy?

An hour later, Jane's image appeared all over the Net, the TV, the wallboards. Her words had been edited to appear that she was a supporter, perhaps even a member, of The Group. But of course we had anticipated this. The moment our van left the warehouse, the first of the pre-emptory spots I'd prepared aired everywhere. They featured news avatar CeeCee Collins, who was glad for the scoop, interviewing Jane about her meeting. Dedicated actress preparing for a role, willing to take any personal risk for art, not a personal believer in breaking the law but valuing open discourse on this important issue, and so forth. The spots cost us a huge amount of money. They were worth it. Not only was the criticism defused, but the publicity for the upcoming movie, which started principal photography in less than a month, was beyond price.

I didn't watch my spots play. Nor was I there when the FBI, CIA, HPA, etc. paid Jane the expected visit to both "debrief" her and/or threaten her with arrest for meeting with terrorists. But I didn't need to be there. Before our meeting, I'd gotten Jane credentials under the Malvern-Murphy Press Immunity Act, plus Everett Murphy as her more-than-capable lawyer. Everett monitored the interviews and I stayed in bed under a painkiller. The FBI, CIA, HPA wanted to meet with me, too, of course, once Jane told them I'd been present. They had to wait until I could see them. I didn't mind their cooling their heels as they waited for me, not at all.

Why are you so opposed to genemods? Jane had asked me once, and only once, not looking at me as she said it. She meant, *Why you, especially?* Usually I answered Jane, trusted Jane, but not on this. I told her the truth: *You wouldn't understand.* To her credit, she hadn't been offended. Jane was smart enough to know what she didn't know.

Now, on my lovely pain patch, I floated in a world where she and I walked hand in hand through a forest the green of her filmy skirt, and she had to crane her neck to smile up at me.

The next few days, publicity for the picture exploded. Jane did interview after interview: TV, LinkNet, robocam, print, holonews. She glowed with the attention, looking ten years younger. Some of the interviewers and avatars needled her, but she stuck to the studio line: This is a movie about people, not polemics. *Future Perfect* is not really about genetic engineering. It will be an honest examination of eternal verities, of our shared frailty and astonishing shared strength, of what makes us human, of blah blah blah, that just happens to use Arlen's syndrome as a vehicle. The script was nearly finished and it would be complex and realistic and blah blah blah.

"Pro or con on genemods?" an exasperated journalist fi-

nally shouted from the back of the room.

Jane gave him a dazzling smile. "Complex and realistic," she said.

Both the pros and the cons would be swarming into the theater, unstoppable as lemmings.

I felt so good about all of this that I decided to call Leila. I needed to be in a good mood to stand these calls. Leila wasn't home, letting me get away with just a message, which made me feel even better.

Jane, glowing on camera, was wiping a decade years of cinematic obscurity with *Future Perfect*. I couldn't wipe out my fifteen years of guilt that easily, nor would I do so even if I could. But I was still glad that Leila wasn't home.

Jane had promised that Friday's role-prep interview would be easier on me. She was wrong.

The Barrington twins lived with their parents and teen-age sister in San Luis Obispo. Jane's pilot obtained clearance to land on the green-velvet Barrington lawn, well behind the estate's heavily secured walls. I wouldn't have to walk far.

"Welcome, Miss Snow. An *honor*." Frieda Barrington was mutton dressed as lamb, a fiftyish woman in a brief skirt and peek-a-boo caped sweater. Slim, toned, tanned, but the breasts doing the peek-a-booing would never be twenty again, and her face had the tense lines of those who spent most of their waking time pretending not to be tense.

Jane climbed gracefully from the flyer and stood so that her body shielded my awkward descent. I seized the grab bar, sat on the flyer floor, fell heavily onto the grass, and scrambled to my feet. Jane moved aside, her calf-length skirt—butter yellow, this time—blowing in the slight breeze. "Call me Jane. This is my manager, Barry Tenler."

Frieda Barrington was one of Those. Still, she at least tried to conceal her distaste. "Hello, Mr. Tenler."

"Hi." With any luck, this would be the only syllable I had to address to her.

We walked across through perfect landscaping, Frieda supplying the fund of inane chatter that such women always have at their disposal. The house had been built a hundred years earlier for a silent-film star. Huge, pink, gilded at windows and doors, it called to mind an obese lawn flamingo. We entered a huge foyer floored in black-and-white marble, which managed to look less Vermeer than checkerboard. A sulky girl in dirty jeans lounged on a chaise longue. She stared at us over the garish cover of a comic book.

"Suky, get up," Frieda snapped. "This is Miss Snow and her manager Mr., uh, Tangler. My daughter Suky."

The girl got up, made an ostentatious and mocking curtsey, and lay down again. Frieda made a noise of outrage and embarrassment, but I felt sorry for Suky. Fifteen—the same age as Ethan — plain of face, she was caught between a mother who'd appropriated her fashions and twin sisters who appropriated all the attention. Frieda would be lucky if Suky's rebellion stopped at mere rudeness. I made her a mock little bow to match her curtsey, and watched as her eyes widened with surprise. I grinned.

Frieda snapped, "Where are the twins?"

Suky shrugged. Frieda rolled her eyes and led us through the house.

They were playing on the terrace, a sun-shaded sweep of weathered stone with steps that led to more lawn, all backed by a gorgeous view of vineyards below the Sierra

Madres. Frieda settled us on comfortable, padded chairs. A robo-server rolled up, offering lemonade.

Bridget and Belinda came over to us before they were called. "Hello!" Jane said with her melting smile, but neither girl answered. Instead, they gazed steadily, unblinkingly at her for a full thirty seconds, and then did the same with me. I didn't like it, or them.

Arlen's Syndrome, like all genetic tinkering, has side effects. No one knows that better than I. Achondroplasia dwarfism is the result of a single nucleotide substitution in the gene FGFR3 at codon 380 on chromosome 4. It affects the growth bones and cartilage, which in turn affects air passages, nerves, and other people's tolerance. Exactly which genes were involved in Arlen's were a trade secret, but the modifications undoubtedly spread across many genes, with many side effects. But since only females could be genemod for Arlen's, the X chromosome was one of those altered. That much, at least, was known.

The two eleven-year-old girls staring at me so frankly were small for their age, delicately built: fairy children. They had white skin, silky fair hair cut in short caps, and eyes of luminous gray. Other than that, they didn't look much alike, fraternal twins rather than identical. Bridget was shorter, plumper, prettier. From a Petri-dishful of Frieda's fertilized eggs, the Barringtons had chosen the most promising two, had them genemoded for Arlen's Syndrome, and implanted them in Frieda's ageing but still serviceable womb. The loving parents, both exhibitionists, had splashed across the world-wide media every last detail — except where and how the work had been done. Unlike Rima Ridley-Jones, the Arlen's child that Jane had spoken with last week, these two were carefully manufactured celebrities.

Jane tried again. "I'm Jane Snow, and you're Bridget

and Belinda. I'm glad to meet you."

"Yes," Belinda said, "you are." She looked at me. "But you're not."

There was no point in lying. Not to them. "Not particularly."

Bridget said, with a gentleness surprising in one so young, "That's okay, though."

"Thank you," I said.

"*I* didn't say it was okay," Belinda said.

There was no answer to that. The Ridley-Jones child hadn't behaved like this; in addition to shielding her from the media, her mother had taught her manners. Frieda, on the other hand, leaned back in her chair like a spectator at a play, interested in what her amazing daughters would say next, but with anxiety on overdrive. I had the sense she'd been here before. Eleven-year-olds were no longer adorable, biddable toddlers.

"You'll never get it," Belinda said to me, at the same moment that Bridget put a hand on her sister's arm. Belinda shook it off. "Let me alone, Brid. He should know. They all should know." She smiled at me and I felt something in my chest recoil from the look in her gray eyes.

"You'll never get it," Belinda said to me with that horrible smile. "No matter what you do, Jane will never love you. And she'll always hate it when you touch her even by mistake. Just like she hates it now. Hates it, hates it, hates it."

It started with a dog.

Dr. Kenneth Bernard Arlen, a geneticist and chess enthusiast, owned a toy poodle. Poodles are a smart breed. Arlen played chess twice a week in his Stanford apartment with Kelson Hughes from Zoology. Usually they played three, four, or five games in a row, depending on how careless Hughes got with his end game. Cosette lay on the rug, dozing, until checkmate of the last game, when she always began barking frantically to protest Hughes's leaving. The odd thing was that Cosette began barking *before* the men rose, as they replaced the chessmen for what might, after all, have been the start of just another game. How did she know it wasn't?

Hughes assumed pheromones. He, or Arlen, or both, probably gave off a different smell as they decided to call it a night. Pheromones were Hughes's field of research; he'd done significant work in mate selection among mice based on smell. He had a graduate student remove the glomeruli from adult dogs and put them through tests to see how various of their learned responses to humans changed. The responses didn't change. It wasn't pheromones.

Now not only Hughes but also Arlen was intensely intrigued. The Human Genome Project had just slid into Phase 2, discovering which genes encoded for what proteins, and how. Arlen was working with Turner's Syndrome, a disorder in which females were born missing all or part of one of their two X chromosomes. The girls had not only physical problems but social ones; they seemed to have trouble with even simple social interactions. What interested Hughes was that Turner Syndrome girls with an intact paternal X gene, the one inherited from the father, managed far better socially than those with the maternal X functioning. Something about picking up social cues was coded for genetically, and on the paternal X.

Where else did social facility reside in the genome? What cues of body language, facial expression, or tone of voice was Cosette picking up? Somehow the dog knew that when Hughes and Arlen set the chessmen in place, this wasn't the start of a new game. Something, dictated at least in part by Cosette's genes, was causing processes in her poodle brain. After all, Hughes's dog, a big dumb Samoyed, never seemed to anticipate anything. Snowy was continually surprised by gravity.

Arlen found the genes in dogs. It took him ten years, during which he failed to get tenure because he wouldn't publish. After Stanford let him go, he still didn't publish. He found the genes in humans. He still didn't publish. Stone broke, he was well on the way to bitter and yet with his idealism undimmed—an odd combination, but not unknown among science fanatics. Inevitably, he crossed paths with people even more fanatical. Kenneth Bernard Arlen joined forces with off-shore backers to open a fertility clinic that created super-empathic children.

Empathy turns up early in some children. A naturally empathic nine-month-old will give her teddy bear to another child who is crying; the toddler senses how bad the other child feels. People who score high in perceiving others' emotions are more popular, more outgoing, better adjusted, more happily married, more successful at their jobs. Arlen's Syndrome toddlers understood—not verbally, but in their limbic systems—when Mommy was worried, when Daddy wanted them to go potty, that Grandma loved them, that a stranger was dangerous.

If his first illegal, off-shore experiments with human germ lines had resulted in deformities, Arlen would have been crucified. There were no deformities. Prospective clients loved the promise of kids who actually understood how *parents* felt. By six or seven, Arlen's Syndrome kids could, especially if they were bright, read an astonishing array of non-verbal signals. By nine or ten, it was impossible to lie to them. As long as you were honest and genuinely had their best interests in mind, the children were a joy to live with: sensitive, cooperative, grateful, aware.

And yet here was Belinda Barrington, staring at me from her pale eyes, and I didn't need a genetic dose of super-empathy to see her glee at embarrassing me. I couldn't look at Jane. The blood was hot in my face.

Frieda said, sharply and hopelessly, "Belinda, that's not nice."

"No, it's not," Bridget said. She frowned at her sister, and Belinda actually looked away for a moment. Her twin had some childish control over Belinda, and her mother didn't. "Tell him you're sorry."

"Sorry," Belinda muttered, unconvincingly. So they could lie, if not be lied to.

Frieda said to Jane, "This is new behavior. I'm sure it's just a phase. Nothing you'd want to include in your project!"

Belinda shot her mother a look of freezing contempt.

Jane took control of the sorry situation. Sparing me any direct glance, she said to Belinda, "Did anybody tell you why I want to talk to you girls?"

"No," Belinda said. "You're not a reporter."

"I'm a movie actress."

Bridget brightened. "Like Kylie Kicker?" Apparently Arlen's Advantage did not confer immunity to inane kiddie pop culture.

"Not as young," Jane smiled, "or as rich. But I'm making a movie about the lives that girls like you might have when you're grown up. That's why I want to get to know you a little bit now. But only if it's okay with you."

The twins looked at each other. Neither spoke, but I had the impression that gigabytes passed between them. Frieda said, "Girls, I hope you'll cooperate with Miss Snow. She—"

"No, you don't," Belinda said, almost absently. "You

don't like her. She's too pretty. But *we* like her."

Frieda's face went a mottled maroon. Bridget, her plump features alarmed, put a hand on her mother's arm. But Frieda shook it off, started to say something, then abruptly stood and stalked into the house. Bridget made a move to follow but checked herself. To me—*why?*—she said apologetically, "She wants to be alone a little while."

"You should go with her," Belinda said, and I didn't have to be told twice. These kids gave me the creeps.

Not that even they, with their overpraised empathy, could ever understand why.

In the foyer, Suky still lay on the chaise longue with her comic book. There was no sign of her mother. The other chairs were all mammoth leather things, but a low antique bench stood against one wall and I clambered painfully onto it and called a cab. I would have to walk all the way to the front gate to meet it, but the thought of going back in the flyer with Jane was unbearable. I closed my eyes and leaned my head against the wall. My back and legs ached, but nothing compared to my heart.

It wasn't the words Belinda had said. Yes, I loved Jane and yes, that love was hopeless. I already knew that and so must Jane. How could she not? I was with her nearly every day; she was a woman sensitive to nuance. I knew she hated my accidental touch, and hated herself for that, and could help none of it. Three of Jane's husbands had been among the best-looking men on the planet. Tall, strong, straight-limbed. I had seen Jane's flesh glow rosy just because James or Karl or Duncan was in the same room with her. I had felt her hide her recoil from me.

"*Sticks and stones can break my bones but words can never hurt me.*" How often as a child had I chanted that to myself after another in the endless string of bullies had taunted me? *Short Stuff, Dopey, Munchkin, Big Butt,*

Mighty Midget, Oompa Loompa, cripple…. Belinda hadn't illuminated any new truth for anybody. What she *had* done was speak it aloud.

"*Give sorrow words*"—but even Shakespeare could be as wrong as nursery chants. Something unnamed could, just barely, be ignored. Could be kept out of daily inter-action, could almost be pretended away. What had been "given words" could not. And now tomorrow and the next day and the day after that, Jane and I would have to try to work together, would avoid each other's eyes, would each tread the dreary internal treadmill: Is he/she upset? Did I brush too close, stay too far away, give off any hurtful signal… *For God's sake, leave me alone!*

Speech doesn't banish distance; it creates it. And if—

"Bitches, aren't they?" a voice said softly. I opened my eyes. Suky stood close to my bench. She was taller than I'd thought, with a spectacular figure. No one would ever notice, not next to the wonder and novelty of the twins.

In my shamed confusion, I blurted out the first thing that came into my mind. "Belinda is, Bridget isn't."

"That's what you think." Suky laughed, then laid her comic book on the bench. "You need this, dwarf." She vanished into some inner corridor.

I picked up the comic. It was holo, those not-inex-pensive e-graphics with chips embedded in the paper. Four panels succeeded each other on each page, with ev-ery panel dramatizing the plot in ten-second bursts of shifting light. The title was "Knife Hack," and the story seemed to concern a mother who carves up her infants with a maximum amount of blood and brain spatter.

Arlen's Syndrome kids: a joy to live with, sensitive and cooperative and grateful and aware.

Just one big happy family.

But sometimes the universe gives you a break. The next day I had a cold. Nothing serious, just a stuffy nose and sore throat, but I sounded like a rusty file scraping on cast iron, so I called in sick to my "office" at Jane's estate. Her trainer answered. "*What?*"

"Tell Jane I won't be in today. Sick. And remind her to—"

"I'm not your errand boy, Barry," he answered hotly. We stared at each other's comlink images in mutual dislike. Dino Carrano was the trainer-to-the-stars-of-the-moment-before-this-one, an arrogant narcissist who three times a week tortured Jane into perfect abs and weeping exhaustion. Like Ishmael, he was without the prescience to realize that his brief vogue had passed and that Jane kept him on partly from compassion. He stood now in her deserted exercise room.

"Why are you answering the phone? Where's Catalina?"

"Her grandmother in Mexico died. Again. And before you ask, Jose is supervising the grounds crew and Jane is in the bathroom, throwing up. Now you know everything. Bye, Barry."

"Wait! If she's throwing up because you pushed her too hard again, you Dago bastard—"

"Save your invective, little man. We haven't even started the training session yet, and if we don't train by tomorrow, her ass is going to drop like a duffel bag. For today she just ate something bad." He cut the link.

My stomach didn't feel too steady, either. Had it been the Barrington lemonade? I made it to the bathroom just in time. But afterward I felt better, decided to not call my doctor, and went to bed. If Jane was sick, Catalina would cancel her appointments. No, Catalina was in Mexico... *not my problem.*

But all Jane's problems were mine. Without her, I had my own problems—Leila, Ethan — but no actual life.

Nonetheless, I forced myself to stay in bed, and eventually I fell asleep. When I woke, six hours later, my throat and stomach both felt fine. A quick call discovered that Catalina had returned from Mexico, sounding suspiciously unbereaved. But she was efficient enough when she was actually in the country, and I decided I didn't need to brief Jane on tomorrow's schedule. That would buy me one more day. I would take a relaxing evening. A long bath, a glass of wine, another postponement of talking to Leila. The industry news on *Hollywood Watch*.

The local news came on first. Ishmael's body had been found in a pond in the Valley.

"…and weighted with cement blocks. Cause of death was a single gunshot wound to the head, execution style," said the news avatar, a CGI who looked completely real except that she had no faulty camera angles whatsoever. I stared at the photo of Ishmael's handsome face on the screen beside her. "Apparently the murderers were unaware that construction work would start today at the pond site, where luxury condos will be built by—"

Ishmael's name was Harold Sylvester Ehrenreich. Failed actor, minor grifter, petty tax evader, who had dropped out of electronic sight eight months ago.

"Anyone having any information concerning—"

I was already on the comlink. "Jane?"

"I just called the cops. They're on their way over." She looked tired, drawn, within five years of her actual age. Her voice sounded as raspy as mine had been. "I was just about to call you. Barry, if this endangers the picture—"

"It won't," I said. Thirty years a star, and she still didn't understand how the behind-the-scenes worked. "It will *make* the picture. Did you call Everett?"

"He's on his way."

"Don't say a word until both he and I get there. Not a word, Jane, not one. Can you send the flyer for me?"

"Yes. Barry—was he killed because of my interview?"

"There's no way to know that," I said, and all at once was profoundly grateful that it was true. I didn't care if Ishmael was alive, dead, or fucking himself on Mars, but Jane was built differently. People mattered to her, especially the wounded-bird type. It was how she'd ended up married to three of her four husbands and the fourth, the Alpha-Male Producer, had been in reaction to the second, the alcoholic failed actor. Catalina, Jane's housekeeper and social secretary, was another of her wounded birds. So, in his own perverse way, was her trainer.

Maybe that was why Jane had ended up with me as well.

But I could tell that neither me nor Belinda's cruel words were on Jane's mind just now. It was all Ishmael, and that was good. Ishmael would get us safely past our personal crisis. Even murder has its silver lining.

As the flyer set down on Jane's roof, I saw the media already starting to converge. Someone must have tipped them off, perhaps a clerk at the precinct. An unmarked car was parked within Jane's gates, with two vans outside and another flyer approaching from L.A. Catalina let me in, her dark eyes wide with excitement. "*La policia*—"

"I know. Is Everett Murphy here?"

"Yes, he—"

"Bring in coffee and cake. And make the maids draw all the curtains in the house, *immediately*. Even the bedrooms. There'll be robocams." I wanted pictures and information released on my schedule, not that of flying recorders.

A man and a woman sat with Jane and Everett at one end of her enormous living room, which the decorator had done in swooping black curves with accents of screaming purple. The room looked nothing like Jane, who used it only for parties. She'd actually defied the decorator, who was a Dino-Carrano-bully type but not a wounded bird, and done her private sitting room in English country house. But she hadn't taken the detectives there. I could guess why: she was protecting her safe haven. Catalina rushed past me like a small Mexican tornado and dramatically pushed the button to opaque the windows. They went deep purple, and lights flickered on in the room. Catalina raced out.

"Barry," Jane said. She looked even worse than on comlink, red nose and swollen eyes and no make-up. I hoped to hell that neither cop was optic wired. "This is Detective Lopez and Detective Miller from the LAPD. Officers, my manager Barry Tenler."

They nodded. Both were too well-trained to show curiosity or distaste, but they were there. I always know. In her sitting room Jane kept a low chair for me, but here I had to scramble up onto a high black sofa that satisfied the decorator desire for "an important piece." I said, "You can question Miss Snow now, but please be advised that she has already spoken with the FBI and HPA, and that both Mr. Murphy and I reserve the right to advise her to not answer."

The cops ignored this meaningless window dressing. But I'd accomplished what I wanted. Dwarfs learn early that straightforward, multisyllabic, take-no-shit talk will sometimes stop average-sizers from treating us like children. Sometimes.

Officer Lopez began a thorough interrogation: How had she arranged the meeting with The Group? When?

What contact had she had between the initial one and the meeting? Who had taken her to the meeting? Who else had accompanied her? When they found out that it had been me, Lopez got the look of a man who knows he's screwed up. "*You* were there, Mr. Tenler?"

"I was."

"You'll have to go with Officer Miller into another room," Lopez said. He stared at me hard. Witnesses were always questioned separately, and even if it hadn't crossed his mind that someone like me was a witness, he suspected it had crossed mine. Which it had. If law-enforcement agencies weren't given to so many turf wars, the LAPD would already know I'd been in that grimy basement. Or if Lopez hadn't fallen victims to his own macho assumptions. *You? She took a lame half-pint like* you *to protect her?*

"Everett is my lawyer, too," I said.

"You go with Officer Miller. Mr. Murphy will join you when I'm finished with Miss Snow." Lopez's formality barely restrained his anger.

Following Officer Miller to the media room, it occurred to me—pointlessly—that Belinda would have known immediately that I'd been withholding something.

It seemed obvious to me, as it probably was to the cops, that Ishmael had been killed by The Group. Narcissistic, bombastic, unreliable, he must have screwed up royally. Was Ms. Resentful dead, too? The bodyguard with the assault rifle? The boy who'd guided us through the warehouse?

The Group was trying to combine idealism, profit-making, and iron control. That combination never worked. I would say that to Officer Lopez, except that there was little chance he would take it seriously. Not from me.

✧

The media spent a breathless three or four days on the story ("Famous Actress Questioned About Genemod Murder! What Does Jane Know?") Then a United States senator married a former porn star named Candy Alley and the press moved on, partly because it was clear that Jane didn't know anything. I'd positioned her as cooperative, concerned, committed to her art, and bewildered by the killing. Opinion polls said the public viewed her favorably. She increased her name recognition six hundred percent among eighteen-to-twenty-four-year-olds, most of whom watched only holos and had never seen a Jane Snow picture. Publicity is publicity.

She got even more of it by spending so much time with the Barrington twins. Everybody liked this except me. Frieda liked the press attention (at least, such press as wasn't staking out the senator and his new pork barrel). The twins liked Jane. She liked caring for yet more wounded birds, which was what she considered them. Her thinking on this escaped me; these were two of the most pampered children in the known universe. But Jane was only filling time, anyway, until the script was finished. And to her credit, she turned down the party invitations from the I'm-more-important-than-you A-list crowd that had ignored her for a decade. I'd urged her to turn down social invitations in order to create that important aura of non-attainable exclusivity. Jane turned them down because she no longer considered those people to be friends.

As for me, I worked at home on the hundreds of pre-photography details. Before I could finally reach Leila, she called me.

"Hey, Barry."

"Hey, Leila." She didn't look good. I steeled myself to ask. "How is he?"

"Gone again." Exhaustion pulled at her face. "I called the LAPD but they won't do anything."

"He'll come home again," I said. "He always does."

"Yeah, and one of these days it'll be in a coffin."

I said nothing to that, because there was nothing to say.

Leila, however, could always find something. "Well, if he does come home in a coffin, then you'll be off the hook, won't you? No more risk of embarrassing you or the gorgeous has-been."

"Leila—"

"Have a good time with your big shot Hollywood friends. I'll just wait to hear if this time the son you deformed really is dead."

She hung up on me.

✧

Leila and I met at a Little People of America convention in Denver. She was one of the teenage dwarfs dancing joyously, midriff bared and short skirt flipping, at the annual ball. I thought she was the most beautiful thing I'd ever seen: red hair and blue eyes, alive to her fingertips. I was eighteen years older than she, and everyone at the convention knew who I was. High-ranking aide to a candidate for the mayor of San Francisco. Smart, successful, sharply dressed. Local dwarf makes good. More mobile then, I asked her to dance. Six months later we married. Six months after that, while I was running the campaign for a gubernatorial candidate, Leila accidentally got pregnant.

Two dwarfs have a twenty-five-percent chance of conceiving an average-sized child, a fifty percent chance of a dwarf, and a twenty-five percent of a double-dominant, which always dies shortly after birth. Leila and I had never discussed these odds because, like most dwarfs, we planned on the *in vitro* fertilization that permits cherry-picking embryos. But Leila got careless with her pills. She knew immediately that she was pregnant, and even before the zygote had implanted itself in her uterus wall, testing showed that the fetus had a "normal" FGFR3 gene. I panicked.

"I don't want to have an average-sized kid," I told Leila. "I just *don't*."

"And I don't want to have an abortion," Leila said. "It's not that I'm politically opposed to abortion. I'm glad to have the choice, but... Barry, I...I just can't. He's already a baby to me. Our baby. Why would having an Average be so hard?"

"Why?" I'd waved a hand around our house, in which everything—furniture, appliance controls, doorknobs — had been built to our scale. "Just look around! Besides, there's a moral question here, Leila. You know that with *in vitro*, fewer and fewer dwarfs are having dwarf children. That just reinforces the idea that there's something wrong with being a dwarf. I don't want to perpetuate that—I won't perpetuate that. This is a political issue! I want a dwarf child."

She believed me. She was twenty to my thirty-nine, and I was a big-shot politico. She loved me. Leila lacked the perspicacity to see how terrified I was of an average-sized son, who would be as tall as I was by the time he was seven. Who would be impossible to control. Who might eventually despise me and his mother both. But Leila really, really didn't want to abort. I talked her into *in utero* somatic gene therapy in England.

In those days I believed in science. The som-gene technique was new but producing spectacular results. The British had gotten behind genetic engineering in a big way, and knowledgeable people from all over the world flocked to Cambridge, where private firms tied to the great university where turning genes on and off in fetuses still in the womb. This had to be done during the first week or ten days after conception. The FGFR3 gene stops bones from growing. It was turned on in babies with dwarfism; a corrective genemod retrovirus should be able to turn the gene off in the little mass of cells that was Ethan. The problem was that the Cambridge biotech clinic wouldn't do it.

"We cure disease, not cause it," I was told icily.

"Dwarfism is not a disease!" I said, too angry to be icy. Waving high the banner of political righteousness. It wasn't a good idea, in those days, to cross me. I was the high-ranking, infallible campaign guru, the tiny *wunderkind*, the man who was never wrong. Fear can present itself as arrogance.

"Nonetheless," the scientist told me in that aloof British accent, "we will not do it. Nor, I suspect, will any clinic in the United Kingdom."

He was right. Time was running out. The next day we went off-shore, to a clinic in the Caymans, and something went wrong. The retrovirus that was the delivery vector mutated, or the splicing caused other genes to jump (they will do that), or maybe God just wanted an evil joke that day. The soma-gene correction spawned side effects, with one gene turning on another that in turn affected another, a cascade of creation run amok. And we got Ethan.

Leila never forgave me, and I never forgave myself. She left me when Ethan was not quite two. I sent money. I tried to stay in touch. I bore Leila's fury and contempt and despair. She sent me pictures of Ethan, but she wouldn't let me see him. I could have pressed visitation through the courts. I didn't.

My gubernatorial candidate lost.

✧

"Barry," Jane comlinked me the night before the first script conference, "would you like to come to dinner tonight?"

"Can't," I lied. "I already have dinner plans."

"Oh? With whom?"

"A friend." I smiled mysteriously. Some inane, back-in-high-school part of my brain hoped that she'd think I had a date. Then I saw Bridget Barrington scamper across the room behind Jane. "Are those kids at your place?"

"Yes, I couldn't go there today because Catalina is sick and I had to—"

"Sick? With what? Jane, you can't catch anything now, the first reading is tomorrow and—"

"I won't catch this—*I* gave it to *her*. It's that sore-throat-and-stomach thing we both had. Catalina—"

"You're not a goddamn nurse! If Catalina is ill—" give me credit, I didn't say *actually ill instead of faking the way she fakes relatives' deaths every fifteen minutes*

"—then hire a nurse or—"

"She's not sick enough for a nurse, she just needs coddling and orange juice and company. It's fine, Barry, so butt out. I'm actually glad of the distraction, it keeps me from thinking about tonight. Oh, I meant to tell you—I talked Robert into couriering the script to me tonight! I wanted to read it before tomorrow. He sounded weird about it, but he agreed."

My radar turned on. "Weird how?"

"I don't know. Just weird."

I considered all the possible "weirds" that the producer could be conveying, but I didn't see what I could do about any of them. I settled for, "Just don't catch anything from Catalina."

"I already *told* you that I won't."

"Fine. Whatever you say."

And it was fine. She was treating me the way she always did, with exasperated affection, and I was grateful. Belinda's poison, flushed out of our working relationship by the flood of feeling about Ishmael's murder, hadn't harmed us. I wouldn't lose the little of Jane that I had.

And the picture was going to be a block-buster.

"It's a disaster!" Jane screamed. "I won't do it!"

Sitting up in bed, I stared blearily at the wall screen. Beneath the image of Jane's ravaged face, the time said 12:56 A.M. I struggled to assemble consciousness.

"What is—"

She started to cry, great gasping sobs that would wreck her face for tomorrow's conference. When had I seen Jane cry like that? When the last husband left. And the one before that.

"I'm coming right over," I said. "I'm leaving immediately. Don't read any more of the script. We'll work this out, I promise."

She was sobbing too hard to answer me.

"Just have a glass of wine and wait for me."

"O…okay."

I cut the link and called my chauffeur. I can drive if I have to, but it's painful. Ernie and his wife Sandra, my housekeeper, live in the guest cottage. They're both achons. "Mr. Tenler? What is it? Are you okay?" Ernie sounded bewildered. They're good people, but I've kept our relationship distant, not given to midnight calls for chauffeur service.

"I'm fine, but I have to go to Miss Snow's immediately. Can you bring around the car in five minutes?"

"Five minutes?" Ernie's face looked exhausted. "Yeah, sure."

"Are *you* all right?"

Surprise replaced his exhaustion. I wasn't in the habit of asking after Ernie's health.

"Yeah, I'm fine, it's just that Sandra and I have both been under the weather. But no big deal. I'll be there in—"

"But if you're sick, maybe you shouldn't—"

"Five minutes," Ernie said, and now suspicion had replaced surprise. What the hell was I doing? I didn't know, either. Painfully I climbed from the bed, tried to flex my aching body, and pulled on clothes. I hobbled out the front door as the Lexus pulled up.

"Here," I said, handing Ernie a pain patch and a plastiflask of orange juice. He stared at me and shook his head.

Jane, in robe and slippers, let me in herself. Her face, red and blotchy and swollen, looked the worst I'd ever seen it. I wanted to take her in my arms, and that turned my voice harsher than I expected. "What's wrong with the fucking script?"

Perversely, my anger seemed to steady her. "It's a travesty."

"Did they reduce your part?"

"That's the least of it! Read it, Barry. I want you to read it for yourself." She led the way to her sitting room. A bottle of wine, half empty, sat on the table. Jane poured herself a third glass as I read, but I wasn't worried about that. Despite her fragile looks, Jane could out-drink a Russian stevedore.

I began to read.

Future Perfect was based on a short story by an obscure writer, which means the studio got the rights cheap. Like much fiction set in the future, it extrapolated from the present, portraying a Mississippi city in which the mayor was an Arlen's Syndrome young woman named

Kate Bradshaw. Kate, empathetic but inexperienced, was guided by Jane's character, an ex-D.A. who was tough, funny, and not above using her mature sexuality for political ends. The story arc brought in prejudice, female friendship, and the choices that politics must make to accommodate radically different points of view. There was a lot of lush Deep South atmosphere. The ending, deliberately ambiguous, featured a knock-out closing speech for Jane's D.A.

The script had moved the story to L.A. The mayor was an evil Delilah who could read minds. She seduced and destroyed men, subverted democracy, had her enemies tortured. Clones were created. Buildings blew up, many buildings. Jane's character was also blown up, a third of the way into the movie. The mayor is eventually shot through the heart by a noble young HPA agent. The body bleeds viscous yellow blood.

"Jane," I said, and stopped. I had to be careful, had to choose just the right words. She had finished off the bottle of wine. I brought her a box of tissues, even though she had stopped crying. "I know it's bad, but—"

"I won't do it." Her flexible voice held the kind of despair that's gone past raging, gone straight into hopelessness.

"This is only the first pass at the script. We can ask for—"

"You know we won't get it."

I did know. I went to the main point. "Janie, sweetheart, this is the only project you've been offered in—"

"I won't do it."

"Jane, you're not—"

"I should think *you* would understand," she said, looking at me directly with a very un-Jane look. No softness, no flirtation, nothing but quiet, unvarnished truth. "This piece of shit encourages hatred. Not just portrays it, but actively encourages it. Arlen's kids are different, therefore they must be bad, evil. More than that — they're the result of a genetic difference, so they must be really bad, really evil, and we should clean them out of our society. I should think you, of all people, Barry, would object to that."

We had never, not once in five years, discussed my dwarfism. She didn't know about Leila, about Ethan. This was uncharted territory for us, and with every cell of my being I did *not want to go there*. She had no right to bring this home to me; it was her decision. Anger hijacked my brain.

"You have no idea what I should or should not object to! Do you think that two weeks spent with a few genetically privileged kids gives you insight into what genetics can do? You know nothing, you're as ignorant and stupid as most of the rest of the so-called 'normal' population. You have no *idea* the anguish that fucking genemods can cause, you think they're all uplifting improvements to mankind, you think that you can just…. Go ahead, commit career suicide! This script is all you've been offered in three years, and it's all you're going to get offered. You're an ageing actress who belongs to another era, a Norma Desmond who will never…. go ahead, tell yourself you're taking the moral high ground! You're standing on quicksand, and I'll be fucked if I let you take me down with you!"

Silence.

She said wearily, "I won't do this script."

"Fine. Get yourself another manager."

I hobbled out to the waiting car and Ernie drove me home.

Jane withdrew from the picture. The studio cast Suri Cruise in the part; she was young enough to be Jane's daughter. Leila called to say tersely that Ethan had crawled home from his latest bout of homelessness. He had a broken nose, a black eye, and a mangled hand. She wouldn't let me come to see him: "How would he even know who the fuck you are?" I didn't insist. The LAPD announced periodically that there were no new developments in the Harold Ehrenreich murder case, and over the next few months, Ishmael's handsome face disappeared from the newsgrids.

Ernie recovered from his bout of flu in a few days, but Sandra's turned into pneumonia and she had to go to the hospital. I visited her every day, to her bewilderment. This was new behavior, but I knew the cause. I had nothing else to do, or at least nothing I could make myself do, and hospital visiting was a distraction. Sandra was only there for four days, but her roommate developed complications and had to go into ICU. She was a frightened old woman with no family. I brought her flowers and chocolate and, when she was a little better, played mah-jongg with her. The game attracted a few other invalids, including a young man dying of one of the few cancers that medicine still couldn't cure. I began visiting him, too. Martin never seemed to even notice that I was a dwarf. Perhaps, as someone once remarked, dying does concentrate the mind, squeezing out everything else.

Every once in a while I reflected wryly that I seemed to have taken on Jane's penchant for wounded birds. But I didn't reflect too hard; hospital visiting was a long way from Hollywood management, which in turn was a long way from the nails-tough political world. I didn't want to look at how far I'd fallen.

Jane, too, seemed to be in wounded-bird mode.

Sometimes, not too often, a picture of her would turn up on some fourth-rate "celebrity watch" linksite, the holo supplied by a desperate paparazzo who couldn't do better. In those shots, she was helping some homeless drunk or paying the bills for a child who owned one ragged dress, or so it was claimed. The holos of Jane with the Barrington twins, on the other hand, turned up regularly on all the news vectors. Frieda Barrington probably saw to that.

In July, Ernie and Sandra quit. "I'm sorry, Mr. Tenler, but we're not comfortable here any more."

"Not comfortable?" I had just spent twenty thousand dollars remodeling the guest cottage.

"No." He shifted from one foot to the other. Ernie has a smaller head and butt than a lot of achons, but he's far from being a proportional, and another job that paid this well for this little work was not going to be easy to find. Not for him, not for Sandra. Where would they go?

"Where will you go?"

"That's our business."

It was such a rude answer that I frowned. Something in the frown broke his reserve.

"Look, Mr. Tenler, it's not that we aren't grateful. You done a lot for us. But lately you're so… We didn't want the cottage remodeled, and I said as much to you. You keep *giving* us things we don't want. And…and hanging around a lot. I'm sorry, but it's a huge pain in the ass."

And I had just wanted to help!

But now Ernie was wound up. "It's like you're trying to control us. I know, I know, you think you're being a good guy, but we…and those calls! They're creeping out Sandra. It's best that we go."

I gave them a generous severance pay-out and hired a Mexican couple, undocumented, who desperately needed jobs. It felt good to help them along. The comlink calls, I started taking myself.

They came once or twice a week. No visual, and the audio came through a voice changer. Routing was via a private, encrypted satellite system, so there was no chance whatsoever of tracing the calls. I thought at first that they might be from Jane, but this emphatically was not her style. Each call was exactly the same:

"Barry Tenler."

"I'm Barry Tenler."

Heavy breathing. Finally, "I know how you feel."

"Feel about what?"

And now the mechanical voice—this isn't supposed to be possible, but I swear I heard it—hinted at pain. "I just want you to know that someone understands. Someone in the same position."

"Look, let me help—" And the link ended.

What "position"? Another dwarf? Another unemployed PR-flack-cum-manager? Another parent of a kid with major genetic problems?

Then I had another mystery because the feds showed up. They proved to be just as elusive as my unknown caller.

"We'd like to ask you some questions, Mr. Tenler."

"What about? Do I need my lawyer?"

"No, not at all. These are just general questions, in the public interest. You'd really help us out."

I blinked. The HPA usually commands "help" rather than requests it, and these were not the erection-jawed types who'd interviewed me after Jane's and my visit to The Group. These two, a man and a woman, were both short, slightly built, mild in manner, deliberately unthreatening. Why? I was curious. Also bored, so I asked them in. Or maybe it was just to see them both perch uncomfortably on my dwarf-sized living room chairs, their knees rising above the cocktail table like cliff faces from a Himalayan valley. "Have you been ill lately, Mr. Tenler?"

"Ill? No. I'm fine." I knew they weren't referring to chronic pain. Nor to chronic self-pity, either.

"No flu-like symptoms?"

"I did have the flu a few months ago, but nothing since."

I could sense the two of them not looking at each other.

"What is this about?" I asked. "I think I'd like to know before I answer any more questions."

"I wish we could accommodate you, sir," the woman said apologetically. She was maybe five-one, pretty, and when she smiled at me, I felt anger swell in my chest. A cheap tactic if there ever was one. *Maybe he'll talk to a woman on his own level…* "Just one more question, please. It would really help us out. Since March, has anyone from The Group tried to contact you?"

"No." If the encrypted calls were from The Group, I didn't know it, and the feds weren't going to, either.

"Thank you, Mr. Tenler," she said winningly, and handed me her card. Agent Elaine Brown, Human Protection Agency.

"Once again, what is this *about*?"

"Please contact us if anything occurs to you, or if you're contacted by The Group," the male agent said. "There's been chatter among our informants."

I knew better than to ask what kind of chatter; he'd probably said too much anyway. After they left, I stared at Elaine Brown's card, wondering what the hell that had all been about.

✦

Two weeks later, I found out. The whole world found out, but I was first.

Another post-midnight phone call, and this time I was not in the mood for it. I'd spent the day at the hospital. Martin, my mah-jongg playing cancer patient, died at 4:43 p.m. The only other person there was his elderly mother, who then fell apart. I had done for her what I could, which wasn't much, arriving home late at night. Three whisky-and-sodas hadn't dulled my sense that the world made no sense. The bedside clock said 2:14 a.m. I snarled at the screen, "*What*?"

"Barry Tenler." It wasn't a question. The screen stayed dark.

"Look, I'm not in the mood for games tonight, so you can just—" Then it hit me that the voice was not mechanical, not masked. A woman's voice, and somewhere I'd heard it before.

"Listen to me, this is a matter of life-and-death for someone you love. Get Jane Snow away to someplace safe and hidden, and do it *now*. Tonight."

"What the—who are you?"

"It doesn't matter who I am. Get her away tonight."

"Why? What's going to—no, don't hang up! You're—"

Where had I heard that voice?

"Just go. Good-bye."

I had it. "You're the woman from The Group. In the warehouse basement." *To date, three thousand two hundred fourteen.* The only sentence I'd heard her utter, and not even a whole sentence. A fragment.

Silence.

"And," I said, as it all came together in my sleep-deprived brain, "you're the woman who's been making those masked calls to me." *I know how you feel....I just want you to know that someone understands. Someone in the same posi-*

tion. "You loved Ishmael."

"They murdered him!" A second later she'd regained control of herself. That a woman like this lost control at all was a measure of her pain. Grief can drive even the toughest person to acts of insanity. Maybe especially the toughest person. She said, "I underestimated you."

I didn't say *People usually do*, because now fear had my chest gripped tight. She was credible, at least to me. "How is Jane in danger? Please tell me."

A long pause, and then she said, "Why the fuck not? But know one thing, Barry Tenler. You will never find me, and neither will the group. And tomorrow morning it will all be public anyway. Tell me, have you ever heard of oxytorin?"

"No."

"Did you get ill a few days after your little visit in March to that warehouse?"

The fear gripped harder. "Flu-like symp—"

"It wasn't flu. Tell me, have you noticed yourself engaged in unusual behaviors lately? Has Jane? Has anyone else with whom you've exchanged bodily fluids, especially saliva?"

I hadn't exchanged bodily fluids, including saliva, with anyone. But all at once I remembered the pre-meeting searches in the warehouse. A man had checked me over, including opening my mouth and moving aside my tongue. His hands had felt unpleasantly slimy.

I was having trouble breathing. "What...what is oxytorin?"

"Nothing that will kill you. The Group is made up of idealists, remember? Idealists who murder anyone who wanders two inches off the reservation." She laughed, a horrible sound. "I know he was dumb and vain, but I loved him. Sneer at that if you will, only you won't, will you? Not you. You're just as enslaved by another beautiful moron. And you can't help it any more than I could, can you?"

"Please...what is oxytorin?"

Her tone lost its anguished cynicism. Relaying factual information steadied her.

"It's a neuropeptide, a close relative to oxytocin, secreted in the brain and the pituitary gland. Like oxytocin, it has effects on social behavior. Specifically, it promotes nurturing behavior. If you give it to virgin female rats, within forty-eight hours they're building nests and trying to nurse any baby rats you hand to them. If you remove it from mother rats' brains, they ignore their babies and let them die. The same with monkeys. It—"

Nurturing behavior. Bringing Ernie and Sandra orange juice and remodeling their cottage. Visiting hospital patients whom I met by accident. Jane, childless, spending hours and hours with the Barrington twins.

"—has been synthesized synthetically for a long time, but the synthetic version has to be injected directly into the brain. That's not practical when you want to permanently influence a large fraction of the population, so instead—"

"You bastards." It came out a whisper, strangled by rage.

"—The Group went with a compound that switches on the genes that create oxytorin receptors. You don't have more oxytorin, you just have more receptors for it, so more of it is actually affecting your brain. Although susceptibility to the genemod will vary among people— like, say, susceptibility to cholera depends on blood type. The delivery vector is a retrovirus, capable of penetrating the blood-brain barrier, but which first colonizes mouth and nose secretions. The—"

"You used us. Me and Jane. You—"

"—desired end here is a kinder, gentler populace. Isn't that what we all want?"

The combination of cynicism and idealism in her words stunned me, because I knew it was absolutely genuine. Again, a whisper: "You can't."

"We did. And if the motherfucking leadership had ever taken it themselves, before they decided Harold was a liability—" She was sobbing. I didn't care.

My throat opened up. I screamed, "You can't just fuck around with people's genes without their consent!"

The sobbing stopped. She said coldly, "Why not? You did."

She knew. They knew. About Ethan.

"I'm telling you this because tomorrow morning The Group is putting the story on the Link. You and your ageing Aphrodite are carriers, and when the press gets hold of that, you'll be inundated, if not lynched. Especially since The Group is saying that Jane Snow cooperated, that this is part of her Hollywood liberal-left politics. Plenty will believe it. And even if they don't, sensationalism always works best when pegged to a few identifiable people. *You* should know that."

"Why are you telling —"

"You don't listen, do you? I already told you why. You're just as fucked as I am. We're alike, you and I, and neither of us ever stood a fucking chance of getting who we wanted. Damn them to hell, all of them…. It always comes down to bodies, Munchkin, and yours has been damned twice. So get yourself and her out of town. Now." The link broke.

I stood staring at nothing for a full minute, for a lifetime. I wasn't even aware of the body she had just mocked. Only my mind raced.

Bodily fluids. Blood, semen, saliva. Jane wiping snot from the noses of the Barrington twins, kissing them, kissing half of the Hollywood press corps in their touch-touch social rituals. And....sleeping with someone? I never asked her. And undoubtedly we weren't the only two that had been infected; that wouldn't be widespread enough. We were just the two that were going to be publicly named.

The weakness of The Group's expensive, individually created genemods for Arlen's Syndrome had always been the very small number of empathic kids it could create. When Jane had pointed this out, Ishmael had gone into his grandiose "ripple" analogy, which explained nothing. But somewhere above Ishmael were people far more knowledgeable, more committed, more dangerous. People with a plan, a revolution for society. The Group had been waging war with the genomes of children as bullets. Now they had moved up to soma-gene engineering, as saturation bombing.

Anger is a great heartener. I dressed quickly, put a few things in a bag, and went down to the car. The kind of encryption that my caller had used was not available to me, and so the comlink was too big a risk. The pedal extenders that Ernie had used in the Lexus, and which Carlos didn't need, were still in the trunk. I installed them and drove to Jane's. I have e-codes to the gate and the house. Within an hour I was at her bedroom door.

What if she wasn't alone?

Deep breath. I went in. "Jane? Don't scream, it's Barry."

"*What—*"

"It's Barry. I'm turning on the light."

She sat up in bed, wild-eyed, and she wasn't alone. The Barrington twins curled up on the other side of the huge bed, lost in the heavy sleep of childhood, their hair in tangles and drool on their pillows. "*What the fuck*—"

All at once my legs gave way. I grasped the edge of the mattress, lowered myself to the floor, and so once again had to look up at her. "Listen, Janie, this is life-and-death. We have to leave here. Now. No, don't say anything—just listen to me for once!"

Something in my voice, or my ridiculous position, got through to her. She didn't say a word as I told her everything that I'd been told. Her feathery light hair drifted in some air current from the open window, and above the modest blue pajamas she wore for this grandmotherly sleep-over, her neck and face turned mottled red, and then dead white. When I finished, I heaved myself to my feet.

"Pack a bag. Five minutes."

And then she spoke. "I can't leave the twins."

I stared at her.

"I can't, Barry. Frieda and John are in Europe, so the kids staying with me this week, and anyway won't they be in danger, too? I must have infected them by now… *saliva*…."

"Catalina will look after them!"

"She's in Mexico. Her aunt died."

I closed my eyes. I knew that look of Jane's. "No," I said.

"I have to! And Frieda would want me to—God, they already get death threats every day! When it's public that they can infect others—"

Nurturing behavior. Virgin rats trying to nurse any baby rats you hand to them.

I said, "It's kidnapping."

"It's not. I'll email Frieda."

One of the girls woke up. She gazed at us from wide, frightened eyes. It was Bridget, the Glinda of the witchy pair. She said in a quavery voice, "Don't leave us, Jane!"

"I won't, darling. I wouldn't."

Bridget looked so small, and so frightened... Then I caught myself. *Oxytorin*. I barked, "No electronics that can be traced. Not phones, not mobiles, not games, not anything. Do those kids have subdermal I.D. chips?"

"No," Jane said. I could see that she wanted to say more, much more, but not in front of Bridget.

Fifteen minutes later, after Jane sent a hasty email to Frieda and John Barrington, we drove out the estate gates, heading toward the mountains.

When Leila was one month pregnant, the ultrasound looked like any other baby. The same at two, five, and nine months. All fetuses have oversized heads, spindly little arms and legs. When Ethan was born, there was no way to tell whether he was a dwarf, except by another genescan. Eighty-five percent of dwarfs are born to average-sized parents, the result not of carrying the dominant gene but of a mutation during conception. Usually the parents don't even realize the child will be a dwarf until the baby fails to grow like other children.

But we, of course, knew. Ethan would be a dwarf. We engineered him to be a dwarf. Then he was born and scanned.

A twentieth-century religious writer once said that humanity needs the disabled to remind us of the fragility of health, and of "the power of life and its brokenness." The nineteenth-century mother of the famous Colonel Tom Thumb attributed her son's dwarfism to her grief over the death of the family dog during her pregnancy. Leila and I had no such spiritual consolations, no such explanations for Ethan's lack of dwarfism. The ones that science could offer were vague: Engineering fails. Genes jump. Chromosomes mutate. Accidents happen. Nature assets herself.

I bought the mountain cabin just after Leila left me. I think now that I wasn't quite sane during that awful time. I'd retired from politics and hadn't yet entered show-business management. I had nothing to do. There are notebooks I wrote then in which I talk about suicide, but I have no memory of doing the writing or thinking the thoughts. Eventually, that time passed. I left the cabin and never went back. Years later I deeded it over to Leila, who would go there sometimes with Ethan when he was small. She told me once, in a rare lapse into civility, that Ethan was happy at the cabin. He chased butterflies, hunted rocks, picked wildflowers. He calmed down up there, and he slept well in the sweet mountain air.

Now the twins did the same, falling asleep on the back seat of the Lexus. Still Jane and I didn't talk. But once she put her hand on the back of my neck. That was a gesture I'd dreamed about, longed for, would have given ten years of my life for. But not like this. Her touch wasn't sexual, wasn't romantic.

It was motherly.

We pulled up to the cabin just as the sun rose over the mountains, an hour before The Group was scheduled to break its story. Jane's skin goose-fleshed as she opened the car door and the cold dawn air rushed in.

"I'm going to carry them inside," she said, the first words she'd spoken in an hour. "They need their sleep. Is the door locked?"

"I have the key."

Mundane words, normal words. While below us, the human race was about to be altered at its core.

The cabin, too, was cold. I started the generator— quicker than building a fire — while Jane, puffing a little, carried the girls one at a time into the bedroom. The cabin is small but it's not primitive or austere; I'm not a fan of either. It has a main room with running water from a deep well, a comfortable bedroom, and a bathroom with full septic system. The original furniture had been sized for me, but evidently Leila had replaced it all. The sofa was hard to climb onto. My legs hurt.

Jane emerged from the bedroom after depositing the last twin, closed the door, and sat down on a wing chair across from me. She said quietly, "You could have let me drive."

I didn't answer.

"Is there a radio here?"

"There was. A satellite radio, the mountains don't permit much other reception."

"Where is it?"

"I don't know. I haven't been here for a long time."

She got up and began opening cupboards in the kitchenette. The counters and appliances, like the furniture, had been replaced, but no new cabinets built above them. Jane had to squat to peer into shelves. She searched the two closets, one of which had not existed when I owned the cabin, then sat down again. "No radio. But a lot of food and equipment. Who uses this place?"

Again I didn't answer.

"Barry, what's our plan?"

I looked at her then. No make-up, barely combed hair, huddled inside jeans and a green sweater that matched her eyes. She had never looked more beautiful to me.

"My only plan was to get you away before some angry mob came after you. People aren't going to like that their brains have been fucked with, and you're a natural target, Jane."

"I know." She smiled wanly. "I always have been, for anybody with a grudge. Why do you suppose that is?"

"Because the perception is that you have it all." I meant: beauty, talent, success, riches. I meant: my heart.

She snorted. "Oh, right. I have a burnt-out career, four bad marriages, and wrinkles that Botox can't touch. Barry, dear, you look tired. Why don't you lie on the sofa and I'll make you some warm milk."

"Don't mother me!" It came out a snarl.

She looked startled, then angry, then compassionate. Compassionate was the worst. "I only meant—"

"That's not you talking, it's the genemod that The Group infected you with."

She turned thoughtful, considering this. Contrary to Ms. Resentful's perception, Jane was not stupid. Finally she said, "No, I don't think so, because I think I would have reacted the same way even before all this started. If I saw you tired and discouraged, I'd have offered some comfort anyway."

This was true. All at once I saw that this was going to be more complicated than I thought. How could anybody determine which behavior was caused by increased oxytorin receptors, and which was innate? It was the old argument, genes versus free will, only now it was about to turn incendiary.

Jane said, "I'm making you that warm milk."

But I was asleep before she could bring it to me.

I woke to Belinda standing beside the sofa, staring at me flatly. "I want to go home."

Groggily I sat up. Everything hurt. "Where's Jane?"

"Her and Bridget went for a stupid walk. Take me home."

"I can't. Not yet."

"*I want to go home.*"

Painfully I climbed off the sofa and headed to the kitchenette. There was fresh coffee in a Braun on the counter, but I couldn't reach it. Hating every second that Belinda watched me, I dragged a footstool from the fireplace to the counter and hoisted myself onto it. A part of my brain noticed dispassionately that I felt no nurturing impulses toward Belinda when she didn't look more helpless than I felt.

The coffee was hot and rich. Good coffee had always been important to Leila. I gulped it down and said, "How long ago did they leave on this walk?"

"I don't know."

She probably did know and wasn't telling me, the brat.

"I really don't know, so stop thinking I'm a liar."

How did she do it? I'd read the literature on Arlen's Syndrome. Subconscious processes in Belinda's malevolent little brain were hypersensitive to six non-word signals: gesture and facial expression, even very tiny movements in either. Rhythm of movement. Bodily use of space. Objectics, such as dress and hairstyle. And what was called paralanguage: tone of voice, rate of verbal delivery, emphasis and inflection. Taken together, they let her read my emotions like a Teleprompter, but she was not reading my mind. I had to remind myself of that. Nonetheless, for the first time I saw the rationale for burning witches at the stake.

She said, "I don't care if you hate me."

"I don't hate you, Belinda." Said hopelessly; I couldn't hide from her.

"I hate you, too."

I took my coffee outside. Leila hadn't removed the low bench in front of the cabin, from which there was a breath-taking panorama of mountains and valleys, a pristine Eden that, when I'd lived here those nine months, had filled me with despair. Eden is no longer Eden if you've been exiled from it. The ghost of those bad feelings seemed to linger around the bench, but I didn't go back inside. Presently Jane and Bridget came puffing up the dirt road, Bridget clutching a mess of buttercups and daisies.

"Hi, Barry," the child said unhappily. She'd been crying. Immediately I braced myself and there it was: the soft desire to reassure her, help her, kiss the boo-boo and make it all better.

God damn it to hell.

Jane sat on the bench beside me. "Go put the flowers in water, Bridget."

When she'd gone, I said, "We need to know what's happening in L.A. There's a library in Dunhill, at the base of the mountain. If you wrap up your hair and wear sunglasses and—oh, I don't know, *act*—do you think you can go in there unnoticed and use the Link? I know I can't."

She looked at the mountain road, which has no guard rails and, in places, pretty steep fall-offs. Jane doesn't like heights. She said, "Yes. I can do it."

"Don't stay long, and don't talk to anybody. Not one word. Your voice is memorable."

"Only if you'd heard it more recently than ten years ago. And in a better picture than my last one. Should I go now?" Again she looked at the road.

Before I could answer, the twins started shouting inside the cabin. Jane rose to her feet as the girls raced outside. Bridget cried, "Belinda, *don't!*"

Belinda said, "If you don't take us home this very minute, I'm going to tell everybody that you touched me in my private place and you'll go to jail forever and ever and ever!"

"No, you will *not*, young lady," Jane said severely. "You just come inside with me this very minute."

Belinda looked astonished. Probably Frieda had never spoken to her daughter that way. I reflected that "maternal behavior" could include discipline. Belinda followed Jane inside.

Had Frieda felt too intimidated by her daughters to reprimand them? Too proud? Too guilty? Had she been too terrified of what they might in turn say to her? I could imagine any of those scenarios, with a child so different from you, so strange, so eerily knowing.

What kind of discipline had Leila given, or not given, to Ethan?

Jane returned from Dunhill in a state of restrained anxiety. Nobody, she said, had recognized her at the library. She'd accessed the Link, watched the news, hardcopied the headlines. It was all even worse than I'd expected.

BIOWEAPON RELEASED IN CALIFORNIA

ARLEN'S WAS ONLY THE FIRST STEP—NOW THEY'RE SPREADING

MUTATIONS!

ACTRESS A PART OF BIOCONSPIRACY SPREADING EPIDEMIC

CALL FOR IMMEDIATE QUARANTINE OF L.A.

RUN ON GAS MASKS, RIOTS, CAUSE DEATHS OF FOUR MUTANTS NOW AMONG US —YOU COULD BE ONE!

JANE SNOW AND MANAGER MISSING SINCE LAST NIGHT

"They're calling it treason," Jane said.

"It is treason. Or something." Bioweapon terrorism. Invasion of bodily privacy. Violations of the Fourteenth Amendment. Medical malpractice.

"What next, Barry?"

"I'm not sure. I need to think." But all I could think about was what might have happened if I hadn't gotten Jane away, if Ms. Resentful hadn't called me. *Riots cause death of four*. And that was without the rioters' zeroing in on a specific target.

"What did the twins do while I was gone?"

"Nothing." They'd played inside and I'd sat outside, pretending they weren't there. Jane went into the cabin.

A minute later she was back. "They're making cookies."

"Fine. Just so long as they don't burn down the cabin."

"We won't," Bridget said, and there they were beside us, having silently followed Jane. Belinda had a picturesque smudge of chocolate on her nose. I did not think that she looked adorable. Bridget added, "Why are you scared, Jane?"

Jane knew better than to deny. "I went down to a town where I could get the news, and some people in L.A. are very angry at another group of people there. It could get violent."

Belinda said, "But why does that mean we can't go home?"

Bridget said, "They're mad at us, too, aren't they? You're scared for us. Why? We didn't do anything!"

Belinda said, "Don't be stupid, Brid. People get mad at

us all the time when we didn't do anything." She looked at me. "Like Barry is mad at us."

Bridget scowled, making her suddenly look more like her sister. "Yeah. Why are you mad at us, Barry?"

"Because I didn't want to have to bring you here. But if I hadn't, you might both have been attacked by a mob now."

Bridget looked scared, but Belinda said, "Naw, we got really good security at home. *Nobody* can get through. I want to go home!"

"And I want you to," I said, which was nothing less than total truth—even as I felt the treacherous desire to comfort little frightened Bridget…*oxytorin.*

Belinda did not look frightened. She was working up to a towering tantrum. "Then take us home! Take us home now!"

Jane said soothingly, "We can't, Belinda. It's not safe. The—"

"It is safe! Daddy's estate is safe! I want to go home!"

Bridget said, with heart-breaking hopelessness, "Belinda—"

Belinda kicked her sister, who screamed and fell to the ground. Then she kicked Jane, who made a grab for her. Belinda was quicker, squirming away, tears of rage on her grimy face.

"Don't touch me! Don't you ever touch me! I hate you, you go around feeling sorry for everybody who isn't you! You feel sorry for Barry 'cause he's all twisted and short, and you feel sorry for Brid and me 'cause you think we're so different, just like you feel sorry for Catalina and the pilot and everybody who's not pretty like you! Well, you're not so pretty anymore *either,* 'cause you're old and you know it and you're scared nobody's going to like you any more if you're not pretty and if you don't do that fuck-

ing movie about us! And you know what—you're right!
Nobody will like you just like I hate you! 'Cause you're
old and not pretty any more and you'll be alone all the
rest of your life! And—"

Jane stood still, looking dazed. Looking stripped na-
ked. But now Bridget was up off the ground and barrel-
ing into her sister head first, a battering ram to the belly.
"Don't you kick me!"

Belinda screamed and the two girls went down, roll-
ing in the scrub grass in front of the cabin, punching and
pulling hair and scratching. Jane sprang forward, trying
to pull them off each other. The sound of a motor made
her, and me, freeze.

And Leila's car roared into sight and jerked to a stop,
with her and Ethan inside.

Empathy means you understand another's feelings. It
doesn't mean you sympathize with them, or respect them.
Hitler's brilliant propaganda minister, Joseph Goebbels,
understood perfectly what the German people were feeling in the 1920's and '30's: insecurity, rage, fear, resentment at the punishments for WWI. He used that knowledge to manipulate their emotions, creating the brilliant
PR campaigns that put Hitler in power and kept him
there.

The Group must have realized too late that Arlen's
Syndrome was not, after all, a guarantee that the world
would change for the better. So they created the virus
that increases oxytorin receptors. Correcting a genetic-
engineering change with another genetic-engineering
change.

I could have told them that does not work.

Ethan got out of the car first, from the passenger side.

Both Bridget and Belinda stopped fighting, got up off the ground, and stared. Ethan's right eye was blackened, and his left arm was in a sling. He scowled ferociously at them, at me, at the world.

He was utterly beautiful.

Auburn hair falling over his forehead, blue eyes, a body that Michelangelo could have used as the model for his *David*. More than that, Ethan had the same quality that Jane did: an innate and unconscious sexuality so blatant that it was like a slap in the face, a challenge: *Come and get me. If you can.* His photos had not captured that quality. Bridget and Belinda were eleven years old, and yet I saw that they felt it, Bridget blushing and looking confused, Belinda scowling back, but with surprise behind her gray eyes. Jane's back was to me. Leila got out of the car and called desperately, "Ethan!"

He ignored her and kept walking. It was me he was moving toward. I stood up from my bench, my heart hammering. Ethan stopped in front of me. I came up to slightly higher than his waist.

"You're my father," he said, with utter contempt. "*You.*"

Leila was running from the car, but Jane was closer. She threw herself between us just as Ethan's fist shot out, and the blow intended for my face hit her in the chest.

"I don't think any of her ribs are broken," Leila said wearily. "She said it doesn't hurt when she breathes, which is a good sign."

Leila and I sat in her car, a three-year-old Ford, each of us holding steaming mugs of fresh coffee. Mine trembled in numb fingers. Jane slept, courtesy of a pain patch, in the bedroom. The twins, subdued now, had been ordered back to their cookie-making, and had actually gone.

Ethan had stalked away into the woods, and I was sickened to realize that I hoped he'd stay away. I was afraid of my son.

"Leila, I didn't realize... I know you'd said, but... Of course, behavior is a complex genetic and environmental phenomenon, and when you interfere with—"

"*Don't*. Don't go informational and theoretical on me like you always do. Just don't!"

"All right."

She turned her face to look at me. "That's the first time I think you've actually heard me when I've said that."

Maybe it was. Information and theory were good hiding places. "And Ethan gets like this—"

"Unpredictably. The psychologist says he has poor impulse control. When he gets upset, there's a major neural high-jacking. You've seen the brain scans with all the irregularities in his amygdalas and hippocampus. He gets swamped with rage, and sometimes he can't even remember what he's done. Not always, but sometimes."

"And you've dealt with this alone for—"

"Since he was a toddler. But you *knew* all this, Barry. I told you."

She had. But I hadn't really heard her, hadn't wanted to hear her. I'd preferred to blame her, as she blamed me.

Leila continued, "When he comes back from the woods, he'll be different. Until the next time. But now that he's old enough to run away...and looking like he does..."

She didn't have to finish the sentence. I knew what L.A. could be for a fifteen-year-old who looked like Ethan.

I said, "Did you two just happen to come up here today?"

"No. Jane called me."

I spilled my coffee. "Jane?"

"Yes. She did what you should have done." Now Leila's anger was back. Anger and blame. "Or didn't you bother to think that Ethan might be in danger once the witch hunt down there fingered you? Which it has, by the way, according to the car radio while I could still get reception on the way up here. Didn't you bother to think that your *son* might make a good substitute target?"

"I didn't think anyone would trace you and Ethan to me."

"Jane obviously did!"

And probably used a private detective to do it. How long ago? Why?

"I'm sorry, Leila. I didn't think you'd be in any danger. I didn't think the media—" I stopped. She knew what I meant.

However nasty the daily world is to dwarfs, there is only one Official Story about us allowed in mainstream media. That's the happytalk Big-Hearts-in-Little-Bodies slant. Dwarfs making good, doing good, being good. Thus is the daily nastiness offset and balance restored to the universe. That the media in L.A. had now abandoned the formula was a strong measure of how much fear The Group had engineered along with their virus.

I said, "This whole thing…God knows I didn't want these twins here, either."

"Where are their parents? Or are you guilty of kidnapping, along with everything else?" Yes. No. "Their parents know the kids are here. They're are on their way home from Europe."

"The Barrington twins, of all kids. God, Barry, you really can screw up royally."

Like I needed to be told that. But I pushed down my anger. This was maybe the only chance I was going to get, and I had to say it right. "Listen, Leila. I want to say something. I know I've been negligent, and I know that Ethan is … I know I had a lot to do with this, because of what I insisted on before he was born. But I want to say three things, and I want you to really consider them. You don't have to, but I'd really like it if you would. First, what I said before is true, even though I picked a stupid time to say it. Behavior is genetically complex, and Ethan's… problems, his brain irregularities, could have happened even if I hadn't insisted on the *in utero* genemod. We'll never know."

Leila made a sudden motion, but I kept on, afraid to stop. "Second, just consider—please consider!—that I tried to help with Ethan and you pushed me away. You were so angry that you… I don't say you weren't justified. But you *did* push me away, and left me, and refused to let me see him, and I think it's unfair that I then get blamed for not seeing him."

"I wasn't—" she said hotly. I put my hand on her arm.

"*Please*. Just one more thing. It's not too late. I want to help, want to do whatever I can, whatever you and he will let me do. If we can get past this anger at each other, finally, and cooperate, that has to be better for Ethan!"

She shook my hand off her arm, but she didn't get out of the car. We sat in silence for a few minutes. I held my breath.

Finally Leila spoke in a different voice. "I don't know if I can. I've hated you for so long… I think…I think I might *need* to hate you. In order to go on."

I knew enough to be quiet.

"Oh, God, I don't want to be that person!" Leila cried. "Barry—"

"I know," I said. "I don't want to be the person I am, either."

She blind-sided me then. "Do you love her very much?"

Only honesty would do now. "Yes."

"I'm seeing somebody," Leila said. "That's part of why Ethan's so angry. He hasn't ever had to share me."

"I'm glad for you, Leila." But I had to ask. "Is he a dwarf?"

"Yes. We met last year at the LPA convention. He lives in Oregon. He's in insurance."

She was smiling, despite herself. I found myself hoping that it worked out for her. She deserved a little insurance. But then, didn't we all.

"I didn't get a chance to tell you before," Leila said. "I brought a satellite TV. It's in the trunk."

Riots had started in South Central L.A. Ostensibly the "mutation plague," which was what the media was calling The Group's virus, was the cause of the riots. But they quickly took on life of their own, with all the usual looting, car burning, rock throwing. The LAPD used microwaves and tanglefoam on the rioters, who then regrouped at different locations and started over again. The press, having been the actual cause of the turmoil with its inflamed reporting, now took on its next role in the inevitable sequence, which was The Voice of Reason trying to calm things down. Talking heads appeared on TV, on the Link, on wallscreens, in holos projected over the city. They explained that the virus was not airborne, needed contact with bodily fluids to survive, and did not cause cancer or suicide or nerve decay or zombie-ism . Nobody listened.

A rumor started that The Group leadership was headquartered in a warehouse by the waterfront. A mob torched it, and strong winds carried the fire westward.

The governor ordered out the National Guard.

KILL THE MUTANT MAKERS said the improvised placards.

Jane was hung in effigy.

Frieda and John Barrington landed at LAX and were besieged by robocams; Jane's picture with the twins had been everywhere in recent weeks. Their flyer finally took off but air space over the city had been shut down and the flyer returned to the airport.

By nightfall the rioting had subsided, damped down by rumors that "muties" were secretly roaming the street, infecting everyone. People fled inside. In several hours of watching the Link, not once did I hear a single reporter or avatar refer to what the virus actually did: increase the desire to nurture. People cared that they had been fucked with, not how.

That was the part of the whole reaction that I most understood.

"Barry," Jane said, "come eat something."

She and Leila had prepared a meal from the canned goods in the cabin. Leila had made a fire in the fireplace. Ethan, who had returned sullen from the woods and stayed sullen ever since, sat at the table with the twins. He'd spent most of the afternoon outside, smoking God-knows-what, while the twins circled him like disintegrating stars around a black hole. Bridget seemed afraid to speak to him at all, but Belinda and he had several long, low conversations during which Ethan scowled a lot. Leila and Jane moved back and forth between table and kitchen, elaborately and artificially polite to each other. I didn't need Bridget or Belinda to tell me what everybody felt. Nobody wanted to be here with these other five people, and there was nowhere else any of us could go.

"Barry," Jane said again.

Belinda said, "He doesn't like you to act like his mother."

I said, "Shut up, kid, or you'll wish you had."

Bridget, wide-eyed, said, "He *means* it, Belinda."

She shut up, glaring at me. Leila glanced my way, puzzled. Ethan raised his head, and I would have given anything for just one moment's of Arlen's Syndrome so I could tell what my son was thinking then.

Bridget said, "I don't like it here with you guys." Her eyes welled, and immediately Jane's arms went around her. "It's okay, Bridget, you girls are just tired. I think you should go to bed right after you eat, sweetheart. Everything will look better in the morning."

Oxytorin.

I was too tired to think straight. But one sentence from Ms. Resentful came back to me: *"Susceptibility to the genemod will vary among people—like, say, susceptibility to cholera depends on blood type."* I'd seen no susceptibility to increased nurturing from Belinda. As she watched Jane hug Bridget, Belinda's look could have withered a cactus.

Leila produced three sleeping bags from the closet that hadn't existed when I'd been here last. The twins were bedded down on the floor of the bedroom. Ethan disdained to so much as glance at his bag, which was laid out in a corner of the living room. Jane and Leila would share the bed. I got the couch.

Ethan and I were the last to go to sleep. I lay on the lumpy sofa, all lights off except for a dim glow where Ethan sat watching something inane on the satellite TV. His beautiful, beautiful face—how had Leila and I created such beauty?—lost its sulky look and relaxed into the smile of a normal fifteen-year-old.

Normal. A word dwarfs don't like and seldom use. For good reason.

But this was my son, and so I made one more attempt to reach him. "What are you watching?"

"Nothing." The scowl was back. It angered me.

"Obviously it's not nothing, or you wouldn't be watching it. So what is it?"

"Don't pull that logic crap on me," Ethan said. "I don't know you." And then—although did even he hesitate before he said it? I thought so, or else I wanted to think so– "Crippled little Munchkin."

We stared at each other across the dim room.

Then I rolled over, wrapped myself in my blanket and my pain, and tried to sleep.

Some unknowable time later, Jane was shaking me by the shoulder. "Barry! Barry, wake up—Belinda is gone!"

I jerked upright and looked at the sleeping bag by the cold fireplace. The bag was empty. My mind went cold and clear. "See if both cars are here."

Of course, they weren't. My Lexus was gone.

"He doesn't even have a driver's permit," Leila said.

She was driving; my legs ached too much. I had made Jane stay with Bridget, who was still asleep. Leila drove slowly in the dark, and as we passed the places where the mountain road dropped off sheerly, she shuddered. But her hands on the wheel didn't falter. This wasn't the teenage dwarf I had married, the girl dancing exuberantly at the LPA convention, the young bride who had blindly accepted my arrogant authority.

"I thought he understood how dangerous it would be to go back home," Leila said. "I thought he *understood*."

"He did. That's why he's going."

She glanced over at me, then returned to her driving, her endless scanning of the roadside. Was that a break in the bushes? Had a car gone off there? Was that a skid mark in the headlights?

She said, "No, that's not why. It's that girl. Belinda. She wants to go home, and I saw her whispering to him all afternoon, and I should have realized…but he doesn't like children! And she's only eleven! I didn't think she could influence him."

Leila was right. I should have anticipated this; I'd seen far more of Belinda than Leila had. Belinda would have known exactly what Ethan was feeling, exactly how to play on his weak spots. She didn't even have to think about it, merely let her instincts take over. Empathy in action.

"Barry, he's not a bad kid underneath. He can be very sweet sometimes. You've never seen that."

"I believe you," I said, wondering if I did. "And the other times—well, he can't help it, can he? It's in his genes."

"*No, it's not.*" The intensity of her anger surprised me, even as she kept on scanning, looking, dreading what she might see. "You attribute everything to genes. It's not true. Genes made you a dwarf, and you think that's wrecked your life, but genes didn't make you so bitter and unhappy. I know that because when we met, you weren't bitter and unhappy. And you were a dwarf then, too. I didn't want Ethan around your self-created misery. I still don't. And maybe he does have some predisposition to danger and anger and impulsiveness, like the doctors say. But he doesn't have to indulge it. He chooses to do that. Just like you choose to be miserable and envious."

"Leila, there's so much wrong with that simplistic analysis that I don't even know where to start correcting it."

"Then don't. I don't need your 'corrections.' You can't—*what's that!*"

I saw it a second after she did. The Lexus, smashed head-first against a tree, which was the only thing that had kept it from going over the embankment.

Leila, younger and with less spinal constriction, was first out of the Ford, running toward the car, uttering loud wordless cries. I followed her, stumbling as my treacherous legs collapsed under me, getting up, trying again to run. Those were the longest seconds—minutes, hours, eons—of my life. Until. I. Reached. That. Car.

They were both alive. Belinda seemed unhurt, mewling in her seat belt. Ethan, who had taken the brunt of the crash—had he turned the wheel at the last minute to save the little girl? — slumped unconscious against the steering wheel. Blood trickled through his bright hair.

"Don't move him," Leila said frantically. "If anything's broken...I'm going for help!"

She ran back to her Ford. I undid Belinda's seat belt, yanked her out, and dropped her on the dark roadside weeds. I could feel her fear, just as she could feel my fury. She shrank back against the fender. I climbed into the passenger seat beside my son.

He stirred. "Mommy..."

"She'll be here soon, Ethan. Help will be here soon."

He said something else, before sliding again into unconsciousness. It might have been, "Fuck you."

Maybe no child, other than those with Arlen's Syndrome, understands how a parent feels. Maybe I hadn't earned the right to even be considered a parent. Maybe, as Leila said, my bitterness and anger would be worse for Ethan than if I weren't there at all for him. I don't know, any more than I know any more what's genetic and what's not. Did Jane go all maternal with the twins because she had more oxytorin receptors, or did The Group's virus make her a good candidate for growing more oxytorin receptors because she'd always had a penchant for wounded birds anyway? *Susceptibility to the genemod will vary among people.*

In the darkness, I sat for a long time beside my injured son. Finally, with great deliberation, I spat on my fingers and gently, gently, pushed them inside his mouth. I felt the softness of his slack tongue, his strong young teeth. Strong teeth, strong long bones. He was not a dwarf. I spat a second time on my hand and did it again.

Overhead, medical and police flyers droned in the dark night When they arrived, I borrowed a cell phone and comlinked Elaine Brown, Human Protection Agency.

A week later, I sit in a Temporary Government Quarantine Facility in San Diego, watching TV. On the other side of the negative-pressure barriers, researchers from the United States Army Research Institute for Infectious Diseases, dressed in Level 4 biohazard suits, go through two airlocks to reach Jane and me. The Barrington twins are here, too, but not Leila or Ethan. Ethan is in a hospital in L.A., and she is with him, along with her boyfriend from Oregon. He flew down immediately to be with her.

They treat us well here. There are endless medical tests, of course, but I'm used to that. Everyone is both respectful and curious. If they're also frightened, I don't sense it, but of course Bridget and Belinda do. Bridget is a favorite with the staff. Belinda wants to go home, although she likes all the attention from Jane. The twins' parents "visit" via Link several times each day. Frieda sometimes has a distinct look of relief. Her kids are behind glass, and she can break the link with Belinda whenever she needs to.

The Link has brought the most attention to Jane. Death threats, pleas for help, fan letters, offers from the

ACLU to sue The Group if any members of that organization can be found, which so far they haven't. Jane would be a high-profile and appealing case. The movie is on again, but not with the same script, or even with the same studio. There's another chapter now to the Arlen's Syndrome story, and Jane has become an actor in that saga in both senses of the word. The whole thing looks like box-office gold.

Jane is not unhappy. If that's not exactly the same thing as being happy, it seems to do.

The Link is also how I visit with Ethan. He had three broken ribs and a damaged spleen, which seems to be repairing itself without surgery. Youthful spleen can do that. We gaze at each other, and sometimes he's sullen, and sometimes I'm impatient, and sometimes he sees me shift on my spine in chronic pain. Or maybe he catches a sadness in my eyes. At such times, his expression softens. So does his voice. He'll ask if I'm okay. When he asks, I am.

Is it wrong to genetically modify human beings? First I thought it wasn't, when I tried to alter Ethan's FGFR3 gene *in utero*. Then I thought it was, seeing both Ethan and the Arlen's Syndrome kids. Now I don't know again. There's still panic out there about The Group's virus, and the virus is still spreading, and eventually it may—or may not—make enough of society more nurturing. In turn, that may—or may not—change society. If enough people are susceptible. If feelings of compassion actually translate into actions of compassion. If the weather holds and the creek don't rise and seven or eleven comes up enough on the dice. This is barely Act One, Scene One of whatever comes next. Chaos theory tells us that, in a system of circular feedback, a small change in initial conditions can cause huge and unpredictable changes down the road. Human behavior is a system of circular feedback. Is Ethan more compassionate toward me because he's growing more oxytorin receptors, or because I'm more open to his (and everyone else's) compassion? How did the same genemod for empathy produce both Bridget and Belinda?

I have no idea. And to tell the truth, I don't really care. I'm supposed to care, ethically and pragmatically, but I don't.

Jane comes into the room and says, "Guess what? The studio is getting Michael Rosen to write the script! Michael Rosen! It's sure to be terrific!"

I smile back. Michael Rosen is indeed a terrific writer, a creator of sensitive and layered scripts that both challenge audiences and fill seats. He's also a handsome womanizer, and Jane is looking more beautiful than ever. I know what will happen.

"That's good," I say. "Congratulations. The movie'll be a smash."

"Thanks to you." She smiles at me and goes out again.

Nothing has changed. Everything has changed. I turn to my computer and get back to work.

Nancy Kress is the author of twenty-six books: three fantasy novels, twelve SF novels, three thrillers, four collections of short stories, one YA novel, and three books on writing fiction. She is perhaps best known for the "Sleepless" trilogy that began with *Beggars in Spain*. The novel was based on a Nebula and Hugo-winning novella of the same name. She won her second Hugo in 2009 in Montreal, for the novella "The Erdmann Nexus." Kress has also won three additional Nebulas, a Sturgeon, and the 2003 John W. Campbell Award (for *Probability Space*). Her most recent books are a collection of short stories, *Nano Comes to Clifford Falls and Other Stories* (Golden Gryphon Press, 2008); a bio-thriller, *Dogs* (Tachyon Press, 2008); and an SF novel, *Steal Across the Sky* (Tor, 2009).

Nancy's fiction, much of which concerns genetic engineering, has been translated into nearly two dozen languages (including Klingon).

In addition to writing, Nancy frequently teaches at various venues: Clarion, writing festivals around the country, the arts center Writers & Books in Rochester, NY, and—most recently—as the Picador Guest Professor at the University of Leipzig in Germany. She lives in Rochester with Cosette, the world's most spoiled toy poodle.

An excerpt from *Daughter of Elysium*
by Joan Slonczewski
Available from Phoenix Pick
and at fine bookstores nationwide

""A major feat"—*Booklist*

"An enormously impressive achievement...A marvelous array of cultures presented in astonishing depth"
—*Kirkus Review*

"A thoughtful, well-crafted novel...Memorable...Intricate...
Rich and Detailed...Touchingly Real"
—*Publishers Weekly*

CHAPTER 1

*T*he sky of the Ocean Moon was blue enough, impossibly blue, bluer than the eye of a newborn. But its surface was not blue at all, as Doctor Blackbear Windclan had expected from the picture-perfect video brochure. As the shuttlecraft bore him and his family ever closer through the clouds, the curve of ocean appeared dusty green, as if a featureless meadow covered the globe. Could this really be Shora, the Ocean Moon?

To reassure himself, Blackbear squeezed the ankles of his two-year-old Sunflower, seated on his shoulders, then he touched the hand of his goddess, Raincloud. Raincloud was a linguist whose training in the tongue of a forbidden world had earned her a job on this free one.

Raincloud returned his look confidently. A goddess of elegant stature, she had the earth-toned complexion typical of their people, the Clickers of Bronze Sky. She carried on her hip their six-year-old Hawktalon, whose cascade of black braids twined in spirals like her mother's. The braids, full of patterned beads, were works of art which Blackbear spent hours redoing each week. Mother and daughter wore their best *rei-gi* garments, as did Blackbear: russet linen trousers that flared like skirts, their hems bordered with embroidered volcanoes and fireweed. A belt tied the garment at the waist—for Raincloud, a black belt.

Blackbear adjusted his turban at his forehead. "This planet looks more like a swamp than an ocean." *Shora,* home of the native Sharers and the ageless Elysians, was an ocean world—the only inhabited world covered entirely by ocean. And yet, the closer came the ocean's surface, the more it looked like a field of vegetation, scraggly green and brown patches with brackish puddles in between. It made his stomach churn, already unsettled from the shifting g-forces of the shuttlecraft.

"Maybe it's Valedon, by mistake," he added, referring to Shora's dryer moon-twin. A country doctor from the frontier of Bronze Sky, a world still largely uncharted, Blackbear distrusted all spacecraft and, for that matter, any contrivance that produced light and speech from no discernible origin.

But he would put up with it. For what he sought on this ocean, countless doctors would give their lives: the secret of immortality.

Raincloud laughed, eyeing the vast "swamp" some ten thousand meters below. "You could herd a lot of goats down there." Her voice clicked crisply, in the language that had earned their people the epithet "Clickers." Clickers farmed the Caldera Hills of the Dark Goddess, beneath a volcanic bronze sky. Twenty light-years distant, yet Bronze Sky was just a *rei-gi* tumble away from here, through a hole in the galactic Fold.

Hawktalon's braids bounced, and she pulled herself up a notch on her mother's back. "Can we really keep our goats after all, Mother? And have room to let the dogs run? Oh please, let's send for the dogs—"

"No," clicked Raincloud. "I told you, we'll be indoors the whole time, within a giant Elysian city."

"Shaped like a bubble, you said," Hawktalon added.

Elysium, the republic of "immortals." Elysians never

aged. They lived a thousand years or more, within their twelve opulent "cellular cities" that floated upon Shora's ocean.

"But even in Founders City," Hawktalon reminded her mother, "people kept dogs." The capital of Bronze Sky was the only city the six-year-old had ever known.

Raincloud looked up from the observation deck and turned toward the back of the carpeted oval compartment. "Servo, please," she called. Raincloud spoke Elysian, the language of the ageless ones, as well as Sharer, the speech of the ocean-dwelling natives who long predated the Republic of Elysium. Most important, she spoke the language of Urulan, the dreaded barbarian world whose missiles threatened the worlds of the Free Fold. Elysian intelligence had recruited her for her knowledge of Urulite. "Servo, please tell us what makes this ocean brown when its sky is blue."

The azure sky was no disappointment, Blackbear conceded, coming from a world whose volcanic dust painted its noonday sky yellow, with hours of blood-red sunset.

"A very perceptive and interesting question, Citizen," came a sibilant voice from nowhere.

Blackbear frowned suspiciously. On his shoulders Sunflower bounced and craned his neck with interest, his stuffed wolf cub doll dangling in his father's face.

"The answer, Citizen," continued the servo voice, "is this. On Shora, by this time of year, the raft seedlings overgrow the entire ocean."

So that was it. Living "rafts" like radial tree branches grew out onto the water. Unlike Elysians, the web-fingered Sharers actually lived outdoors upon the larger rafts.

As the servo spoke, Raincloud murmured simultaneous translation for Hawktalon. This talent had earned the goddess a job as interpreter for the Sharer embassy in Founders City, where Blackbear had studied medicine. Elysium, of course, had Sharer experts aplenty; their treaty with the ocean-dwellers required continual consultation. For Elysian Foreign Affairs, Raincloud would be translating signals from spy satellites at Urulan.

And Blackbear would do medical research, at the Longevity Laboratory of the famous scientist Tulle Meryllishon.

"In just two weeks," the servo voice told the Windclans, "the giant seaswallowers will migrate from the south pole, consuming the overgrown raft seedlings you see below, along with anything else in their path. Despite our best efforts, one or two Sharer rafts are lost each year."

"Lost?" Blackbear exclaimed. "But—what about us?" Elysian cities, like the living rafts, floated upon the ocean, each one a great sphere of nanoplast some four kilometers across. The city of Helicon, the Windclans' destination, lay ahead now, a gleaming pearl set in the seedling-choked sea. The pearl grew steadily larger as they approached. A single dwelling for a million immortal souls; the sight of it took his breath away. Yet even a structure so huge could be swamped by the sea.

"The city of Helicon could be lost, Citizen," the voice added. "Its surface was breached, once, forty years ago. If the leak had not been fixed, the city would have filled and sunk in fifty-three point six days."

Sunflower bounced happily on Blackbear's shoulders. "Snake, Daddy," he clicked. "*Ss-ss*, I hear snake." The sibilant Elysian voice, which the child could not understand, sounded like hissing.

Blackbear asked, "But what happens if—"

"*Snake,* Daddy."

"All right, it's a snake. Now be quiet, Sunny." The child insisted on hearing his pronouncements repeated, to make sure their wisdom had sunk in.

Hawktalon laughed. "Sunny thinks he heard a snake. What a baby. It's not even Snake Day yet."

The servo added, "Does my vocalization fail, Citizen?"

Blackbear said, "No, but—"

"If so, please report my defect to Service Sector Oh-three-twenty in the Nucleus of Helicon, for training. Actually, Citizen, the sinking of Helicon or any other Elysian city is most unlikely; no such event has been recorded in nine centuries since the founding of the Republic. The city's compartments are pressurized at all levels, and a buoyant fluid fills its transit reticulum, like a great living cell. Attention: Helicon's surface lies just beneath us. See the sunlight sparkle on its shimmering dome? Prepare for landing."

An indentation appeared in the city's surface, as if an invisible giant had pressed a thumb into it. The thumbprint deepened and widened, and the shadow of the shuttlecraft fell across it.

At his side, Raincloud clicked, "Strap down again."

The four of them returned to their seats, which automatically strapped them down for safety. Blackbear zipped Sunflower's empty juice cup into his travel bag.

Hawktalon announced, "I'll carry my own bag off the shuttle."

"Sorry, you'll ride for now," her mother insisted. No respectable Clicker adult would walk in public without a child on her back, or his.

Hawktalon pouted, and her much-worn stuffed fruitbat hung listlessly. A bit old to be carried, she would have to put up with it until Raincloud conceived another child. Back home in Tumbling Rock, the clan always had a number of little ones to hold; but here, of course, they had only these two. Clicker goddesses spaced three or four years between children, to prolong the nursing of each.

The craft shuddered to a halt. "Thank you, Citizens, for enjoying my service. A reminder: You will be met at the transit node of Octant Six by your host, Alin Anaea*shon,* mate of Tulle Merylli*shon...*"

Tulle Merylli*shon* was the lab director. Merylli*shon* was not a clan name, for Elysium had no clans. The *shon* name referred to the nursery of birth. Each city had its central *shon,* where the children were born and raised in common.

This arrangement was incomprehensible to Blackbear, for in Tumbling Rock even orphans had extended families. But then, the Elysians could have no children of their own. Immortality came at a price.

The Elysians were sterile. Their lack of germ cells was a side effect of the genetic treatment of their embryos, in the artificial wombs of the *shon.* The embryos, all derived from non-Elysian sources, had to be grown in culture.

What was the link between aging and fertility? No scientist had yet cracked it, but Tulle Merylli*shon* was trying. That was the Fertility Project, which Blackbear had come to work on. There were frontier worlds to populate, new fertile hills to fill with growing families. Few non-Elysian parents cared to produce children who could expect no children of their own. But if the Fertility Project succeeded, every child in the Fold could be born immortal.

Outside the shuttle, the chill air brought a scent of orange and salt from Shora's ocean. A wind shrieked overhead across the lip of the cavity which held them in the surface of the Elysian city.

Hawktalon winced and covered her eyes. "The sun—it

burns, Mother."

"Look away from it, dear," Raincloud reminded her. This sun blazed without mercy through the clear blue sky, untempered by volcanic haze.

The lip of the cavity rose around them and constricted, blocking the sun. Now the lemon-colored disk of Valedon, Shora's moon-twin, appeared against the blue. Then the shuttle lifted off out of the cavity, and the lip soon closed overhead.

The cavity now became an enclosed vesicle, diffusely lighted. Within the vesicle, so small after the expanse of sky and ocean, Blackbear felt trapped. But Sunflower caressed his forehead and leaned forward with interest. "Going downstairs," the child clicked softly.

"Yes, Sunflower, 'downstairs.'" The vesicle was floating downward at about a sixty degree angle, along a fluid-filled branch of the transit reticulum. The flow of liquid carried the vesicle in its path.

"Welcome, Citizens, to Helicon, capital of Elysium, home of butterflies for a thousand years." Another disembodied servo voice. Blackbear's hair stood on end. "Would you be seated, Citizens?" the voice added.

Raincloud said, "Yes, thank you," in faultless Elysian.

Behind Blackbear, a lump of nanoplast pushed up and molded itself into a chair. The entire vesicle must be made of nanoplast, an "intelligent" material. But how could that stuff form such intricate shapes? Similar chairs took shape for the four of them. Hawktalon exclaimed with delight, and the beaded braids jangled about her face.

"If I ever fail to serve promptly, please report my defect to Service Sector Oh-three-thirteen. Now, the latest news. The Urulite Imperium claims that the Valan freighter *Sardonyx* entered Urulite space before it was destroyed. Urulan threatens Valedon itself with interstellar missiles..."

Ghostlike figures sprang up on a little holostage, before the incurving wall of the vesicle. Hawktalon shrieked and clapped her hands. Blackbear shuddered, wondering where such a backward planet as Urulan could have gotten interstellar missiles. What if they hit Shora as well as Valedon? At any rate, the news was bad enough without showing it in three dimensions.

The chair oozed to fit his shape as he stretched. Was there anything in Elysium not "alive," responsive and motile? Or rather, were there any *live* Elysians, other than holo figures?

From the left, another vesicle entered the stream and approached alongside. Its surface touched and seemed to melt in. The two vessels fused, their walls joined and widened to reveal several passengers.

Elysians were small, compact people, rarely taller than Blackbear's shoulder; they were designed to make the most of their living space. Their complexions ranged from pink to brown, one of them pale as cream; their genetic stock, Blackbear knew, included sperm and ova from all worlds of the Free Fold, even Bronze Sky. They wore Valan talars with long patterned trains, now bundled up by pairs of "trainsweeps." Trainsweeps were beetlelike servos, with their six legs poking out beneath their polished shells, scurrying behind their masters to keep the trains in order. Their Elysian masters did not speak or even smile in greeting; a custom common to cities, Blackbear had learned during his medical training at Founders University. Back in Tumbling Rock, however, in the Caldera Hills, if one failed to recognize a passerby, one immediately said hello to make the acquaintance.

The nearest of the seated Elysians wore a train of unusual length, requiring two pairs of trainsweeps to carry the folds of pale green silk. He must have been at least five hundred years old, therefore; she or he, Blackbear could not tell which, he realized with a shock. A goddess, after all, he decided, much embarrassed, adjusting his turban self-consciously. A "woman," an Elysian female, though the Elysian word did not connote all that the Clicker "goddess" did. Her hair fell unbraided to her shoulders, and her talar reached to her sandaled feet. The portion of her train that clasped her back was embroidered with butterflies, deep blue heliconians, their long wings marked by red bars and edged with white.

Each of Elysium's twelve cities took a different butterfly as its emblem; heliconians, for Helicon. Blackbear had forgotten why this was so, but nonetheless he sighed to see something familiar. Bronze Sky, like Valedon and most other inhabited worlds, had been terraformed long ago with stock from ancient Torr. Shora had not; thus the native rafts and seaswallowers remained. But the first Elysians had brought butterflies from their terraformed home world.

"And now—trainsweeps and housekeepers on sale," the servo voice continued. "The very best from Valedon." Shora's moon-twin was well known for the manufacture of servos. "All at The Golden Fritillary..." The shop address went beyond his grasp of Elysian.

"They're selling goddesses," clicked Raincloud mischievously.

Startled, Blackbear asked, "How's that?"

"Well, in Urulite, our word 'goddess' would translate as 'domestic property,' which is what the Elysians have put on sale." A trilingual pun.

"Well," said Blackbear, "we're far from Urulan and its barbarians, thank the Dark One." Twice as distant as Bronze Sky, Urulan had closed itself to foreigners for two centuries, and allowed few of its own to venture out. Fortunately Raincloud would see no live Urulites in Elysium.

"Urulites aren't all bad," she reminded him. Raincloud had studied Urulite with an émigré professor, an escaped slave.

"The good ones leave or die." Like Shora, Urulan had never been terraformed, but its people were as uncivilized as its plated fourteen-legged carnivores. In an age when most worlds traded freely across the Fold, Urulan's goddesses were herded like sheep, and their male warriors fought each other with crude nuclear bombs. They even bred gorilla hybrids as slaves—like Raincloud's old teacher.

Sunflower was tugging insistently at his father's collar. "Doggie," clicked the child.

"What's that, Sunflower?"

"Sunflo' see Doggie. Sunflo' fly down. Fly down, see Doggie."

Blackbear looked down. At the end of the Elysian's bundled train, one of her six-legged trainsweeps wiggled back and forth slightly. "Sunflower, that's not a dog, and you can't fly down now."

"Sunflo' fly do-own!"

Raincloud shrugged. "Let him down, why not."

"Me too!" Hawktalon slid to the ground.

There was no place to run, after all. Blackbear let Sunflower down and watched him toddle off on tiptoe after his sister, both swinging their animal dolls behind them. They inspected the trainsweep, taking in its every move.

Seeing them, apart, in this world of strangeness, Blackbear fought back a wave of anxiety. It was an old fear he had, about losing his child. It must have started years before, at age seven, when he had lost his youngest brother in the swollen river. He barely remembered what

90

his brother looked like, now; whenever he recalled the incident, or dreamed it, it was Sunflower he saw in his arms.

No children. Those Elysians with their unburdened shoulders and smooth complexions, yet they might be eighty, or eight hundred...

Of course, there were Elysian children, Blackbear reminded himself. Raised in the artificial wombs of the *shon*, seeded from the best imported genetic stock, just enough children were born to offset mortality by accident and rare disease. Just enough to fill the jobs the city needed. But not enough for each one to carry one.

"Transit node, Octant Six," said the voice. "Prepare to disembark."

The vesicle had fused to several more vesicles by now, including one that descended from above and had to lower its occupants onto the platform. It had formed itself into a great length of sausage. After some minutes, its rate of flow lessened. Out of the translucent fluid ahead there appeared a white wall, into which the vesicle merged and opened. The Windclan family gathered up their bags and stepped out.

They entered a vast pulsating cavern. Here, vesicles fused to the cavern, while elsewhere new vesicles pinched off, flowing down other branches of the reticulum. The ceiling played a lightshow of butterflies, their long golden wings sporting black spots; another heliconian variant, he guessed. Below thronged the Elysians, their hair neither braided nor bound up in turbans, their trains extending back several meters to their trainsweeps. Countless servos mingled about, tall loud-spoken ones vending drinks and sweets, broad flat ones offering transport, disconcerting little insectlike ones quietly vacuuming the spotless floor. Even overhead, little bell-tinkling hovercraft glided by. And still, not a child to be seen....

It was not just that in the Caldera Hills, the fertile slopes and endless forests needed many hands for harvest, and children were the growth industry of a world with a dozen empty continents to populate, facing floods, fires and landslides along the way. Beyond that—

What was an adult without children? How could one even begin a conversation, without presenting one's off-spring or younger sib? Among Clickers, even children presented their dolls. Could these Elysians *feel*? Could they care about others? Was eternal youth worth the price?

Blackbear thought of his father with prostate trouble, and his last patient, the elderly woman from the next town whom he had treated for kidney failure just before he left home. *Why was aging linked to fertility?* Blackbear hoped soon to learn. The Fertility Project could change everything. Everyone might then have ageless children of their own. It was too late for Hawktalon and Sunflower, he thought with a pang, but then he and his goddess expected another six or seven children.

From Raincloud's back, Hawktalon exclaimed, "Oh, look who's here!"

The trainsweep had left its master and followed behind them. Astonished, Blackbear stared at its polished silver surface, which reflected splotches of gold from the ceiling butterflies.

Raincloud glared at her daughter. "It's the one you were pestering."

"Oh Goddess," exclaimed Blackbear, his stomach in knots. "What if someone thinks we stole it?"

"We *didn't*, Dad." Hawktalon was indignant. "Go away, bad Doggie," she told the trainsweep, but her cheerful tone belied her words.

Raincloud said, "We'll leave it at 'lost and found,'

somewhere. Servo?" she called. "Where's that damned servo voice when we need it?"

He winced, wishing she would watch her language in front of the little boy.

Just then, Sunflower half slid off his shoulder and leaned toward a vendor, a servo shaped like a lamppost attached to a tray of scooped sweets. "Ice cream. Sunflo' hungry."

"No," said Blackbear. "*No* ice cream, that's that." Wherever was that Elysian to meet them, he wondered.

The child tensed ominously. His eyebrows wrinkled, and the corners of his mouth pulled down. Then he let out a wail that caused heads to turn.

Blackbear hurriedly brought him down and rocked him in his arms, but it was no use. Sunflower screamed and flailed his limbs in all directions.

"Sh-sh." Hawktalon covered her ears.

Raincloud was searching around. "Try to spot an 'information vendor.' They look like—"

A ringing bell sounded overhead. It was an airborne hovercraft. The hovercraft landed right in front of Blackbear. It spouted an Elysian phrase which he did not catch. Two servos emerged, emergency lights blinking around their heads.

"Please lay patient on the floor, head raised." A stocky machine, about as tall as Hawktalon, spoke in the soothing tones of a flight attendant. "Some hyperventilation, we see."

The other servo, shaped more like a lamppost, extended two long tentacles snaking around the child in Blackbear's arms.

"*No*," he shouted, adding in Click-click, "get off, by the Goddess!" He bent at the knees, his left foot slid back, then he twisted the grasping servo over in a somersault.

Rei-gi aimed for gentle disengagement.

"Do not damage City property," the lamppost intoned as it rearranged itself. "A fine may be charged."

The stocky servo observed, "The child is foreign, a defective. We are not equipped to treat defectives. We must call reinforcements. Meanwhile, please lay patient on the floor."

"Nonsense," snapped Raincloud. "We'll put *you* on the floor." Raincloud had earned a black-belt, as did all goddesses, several levels higher than that permitted men. "Defective, indeed," she muttered, her eyes dark as those of the six-armed Goddess of the Hills.

"Hai!" Hawktalon swung her hands up in a practice move.

"Pardon me..." An Elysian man stood nearby. "Doctor Windclan, I presume?"

The childless man wore a talar of tawny brown, almost like the sky of Bronze Sky. His train had a border of what looked like autumn leaves, unlike the gaudy butterflies of the other Elysians. Tall for an Elysian, he still had to look up to Blackbear's face. His complexion was smooth as a baby's, yet his impeccable grooming and composure marked his maturity.

"Yes?" said Blackbear hopefully.

With a slight bow, the man added, "I am Alin Anaea-*shon*, mate of Tulle Merylli*shon*. Meeting you is my highest duty; my mate has told me so much about you."

Of course, Blackbear recalled. The Director's "mate" would have to meet him first, an Elysian custom. The same would be true for Raincloud's supervisor, and for any other Elysian they had to meet.

Raincloud nudged him, whispering a phrase in his ear. Blackbear nodded stiffly; it was hard to bow, with the child on his neck. He returned the formal phrase. "My

94

mate Raincloud will hear glowing reports of you." He hoped his accent was not too bad. The word "mate" still bothered him; it could mean either goddess or consort.

"Such an honor," said Alin. "And your... little friend; has he received proper care?"

The child was still sobbing on and off.

Blackbear said, "Let me present Sunflower, my..."

"... *shon*ling," prompted Raincloud.

"And here's Fruitbat," clicked Hawktalon, extending her stuffed animal.

Sunflower buried his face in his father's shoulder, but held out Wolfcub by its tail.

"The defective was hyperventilating," insisted the servo. "The foreigners obstructed our care. Reinforcements will arrive."

Sure enough, a second hovercraft was settling beside the first.

"Your training is defective," Alin calmly told the servo. "First, foreigners require consent for treatment. Second, the patient is clearly a *shon*ling."

The servos immediately drew back. "He is not registered with any *shon*," said one. The lamppost-type added, "Please report our defect to Service Sector Two-seven-twenty."

Immediately the servos reentered their hovercraft and took off. Sunflower was calmer now, just sniffing at intervals. "Bird," he clicked, eyeing the departing hovercraft. "Bird fly away."

"Well." Alin smiled slightly. "Sorry, the medics were only trying to help. If you register your child with the Heli*shon*, you'll have no more trouble." The Heli*shon* was the main nursery-womb of Helicon.

"We plan to register," said Blackbear. "But we've only just arrived."

"I say…" Alin was looking past Blackbear to something behind him in the street.

Blackbear turned. There was the runaway trainsweep still, behind him now, as if carrying an invisible train. His heart sank again. "It followed us out of the vesicle," he explained, much embarrassed.

Alin gave a peal of laughter, like a delighted child; for the first time, the Elysian seemed to come alive as a real person. "I expected you in native dress, but—a trainsweep without a train? Tulle will love it!" His look of gravity returned. "Never mind; its network must have crossed connections and oriented to you by mistake. Just look up its owner and give his mate a call."

Raincloud asked, "Couldn't we just turn it off?"

Alin shook his head. "It might take a while to retrain. Let's get you to your house, shall we?" He motioned them to follow. Blackbear thought of his longhouse on the mountainside, with the goats scampering down to pasture below. "We'll just take the next vesicle, this branch, and tell the servo your address. You'll need rest; we'll get acquainted tomorrow, on the way to the lab. No problem, tomorrow's another Visiting Day for me." The Elysians had a three-day work week, restricted by law. An inefficient way to do business; but then, the immortals could take their time.

Hawktalon clapped her hands. "Oh Daddy, can I go to the lab, too?"

Raincloud answered, "Not tomorrow. You must come with me, to meet important people." Raincloud wanted to show off her firstborn goddess at Foreign Affairs.

"Next week," Blackbear promised. As the long golden train behind Alin passed before him, he suddenly saw that what looked like dead leaves in the border pattern were in fact butterflies after all, anaeans, their crinkled brown wings evolved to resemble litter on the forest floor. Clever camouflage; these butterflies were more than they seemed.

Their Elysian host led them down a "street" that felt more like a tunnel, Blackbear thought. The facades at either side were all shaped like the profile of an hourglass, their foundations curving down into the street while their upper stories arched into the luminous sky-ceiling. The shop windows were wide open, without even mesh screens to keep out insects. Not that he had seen any insects, save for an enormous garden of butterflies; the sight drew his gaze backward as they passed.

"Here's your house," said Alin at last.

Blackbear saw what appeared to be the faint trace of a doorway in the wall before him, at the end of a gently sloping ramp. He gave Alin an uncertain look, trying to muster up the courage to ask the location of the handle. But before he did so, the center of the door pinched in and molded outward, until a doorway had formed, jambs and all. His toes curled within his shoes.

"You'll get used to nanoplast," Alin assured him. "It always startles foreigners at first. Think of it as a sort of modeling clay inhabited by billions of molecular servos. That's what they told me when I was a *shon*ling."

Blackbear smiled despite himself. This Elysian had not forgotten his own childhood, after all his centuries.

"Thanks for your help," said Raincloud. "When should we expect our luggage?" Traveling on Bronze Sky, their luggage had always seemed to end up behind.

Alin paused as if surprised. "Is anything missing?"

Blackbear blinked, then looked inside.

The solid oak dining table, its legs fully assembled, stood in the near room, upon the woolen rug woven by

Blackbear's brothers for his wedding. The curtains, which he had sewn to fit the windows back home and expected to have to redo completely, now hung upon windows shaped perfectly to fit. Raincloud's clan portrait, with her three sisters, twelve brothers, and assorted nieces and nephews, and himself beside her, hung right there on the wall. He had packed it away in three layers of wrapping.

Blackbear felt shock and indignation. Who had dared to go through their things?

Hawktalon skipped through the doorway. "Look—it's our house already!"

"Not bad," Raincloud admiringly told the Elysian. "Your people are most considerate."

"Oh, the house took care of everything."

Blackbear's anger subsided. As usual, his goddess was less particular about interiors than he was. He should be grateful, he realized, for packing and unpacking was the one thing that could drive him and Raincloud to snap at each other. Still, as he went inside to look around, he wondered at the lack of privacy. In Tumbling Rock, no stranger would enter a house unasked.

"The Dark One will need a shrine, though." Raincloud had located the figure of the Dark Goddess, standing most inappropriately at the rear of the sitting room. The black glazed figure, about half height, had the traditional six arms of the Goddess: her lower two hands held a baby to the breast; her middle two grasped a fanged snake at its head and tail, its midsection caught in the Dark One's mouth; and her upper two hands lifted overhead in a gesture of the dance, their fingertips aflame.

Alin said, "Just tell your house to push out another room. You've not yet filled your quota."

"Twelve hundred cubic meters is your quota," said a voice. "Your rooms at present total seventy percent of quota."

Blackbear gave a start, and looked around.

"I am your dependable housing unit," said the voice, "manufactured by the Valan House of Chrysolite. If I ever fail you in any way, citizen, please report my defect to..."

Blackbear's mouth fell open, and a chill reached his toes. He thought, *Even our home has a ghost.*

From the doorway, Alin observed, "The holostage should connect right here. Let's have the news," he called to the house.

A gossamer shell of light appeared in the sitting room, above the holostage. It formed a man, full-size, wearing a talar with cut stones arrayed across his chest. It was the prime minister of Valedon, Shora's sister world, standing right there in the Windclans' home. "The Ministry categorically denies this allegation," the man's voice boomed, too loud for comfort; Hawktalon clapped her ears. "It is inconceivable that any Valan vessel would violate the recognized space boundary of Urulan, or of any sovereign world. Surely the Free Fold will accept our word, the word of a peace-loving democratic society, over that of a state mired in feudal barbarism—"

"Silence, please," ordered Raincloud.

The voice ceased, but the speaker remained.

"Valedon used to be feudal enough, a few centuries back," muttered Raincloud.

A house full of ghosts, thought Blackbear.

The house obligingly tunneled an extra room for the shrine of the Dark One. It also reshaped Hawktalon's bedroom at her impudent request, giving it a domed ceiling like that of the Temple back home. Then it produced their dinner out of a "window" in the kitchen, roasted goat flesh with potatoes, steaming hot, as if by magic. Before Blackbear even looked for a broom, several servos like large cockroaches came out and sucked all of Sunflower's crumbs off the floor.

It fascinated him, yet annoyed him, too. "Those servos will try to do your braids next," he grumbled to Raincloud as he undid his turban and shook out his hair, then slid exhausted into their ready-made bed.

"Nonsense. I'd toss them out, first." Her arms stretched back amongst the braids, and her breasts rose, as beautifully dark as the rich soil of the Hills. Then she reached up and pulled him over on top of her. Suddenly she was as hungry and desirous as the Dark One devouring the snake. They weren't quite so exhausted after all, Blackbear decided.